THE MUD BALLAD

JO QUENELL

PRAISE FOR THE MUD BALLAD

"Jo Quenell's debut novella explores both regret and connection in the weirdest and wildest ways possible. Good times!"

— DANGER SLATER, AUTHOR OF THE WONDERLAND AWARD WINNING *I WILL ROT WITHOUT YOU*

"A whiskey-burn tale of loneliness and regret, Quenell's debut will shove your face in the slop and leave you lucky to see another awful day."

— KATY MICHELLE QUINN, AUTHOR OF *WINNIE*

"A Southern Gothic folk tale steeped in black humour and the occult. If you enjoyed Geek Love, Nightmare Alley, or the works of Joe R Lansdale, you'll love the unique brand of literary madness Jo Quenell has conjured with The Mud Ballad."

— BRENDAN VIDITO, AUTHOR OF THE WONDERLAND AWARD WINNING *NIGHTMARES IN ECSTASY*

CONTENTS

PROLOGUE

Then

Daniel Crabb confronted his brother as they prepared for the evening's show.

"Are you going to do it?"

Jonathan Crabb finished guiding the straight razor down Daniel's lather-laden cheek and rinsed the blade in the soapy bowl on the ground between them, ridding the steel of stubble and foam. "I don't know what you mean."

Daniel scoffed. "Yes, you do. Come on, Jon. I know what you've been thinking. I get it. *Nobody* should want this. Nobody deserves to be us."

Outside their tent, carnies joked over the jangle of calliope. Inside, both brothers wept. Jonathan focused on Daniel's thoughts. A panicked plea reverberated in their collective subconscious—*please, Jon, please don't*—but it was faint. They both knew this moment was inevitable.

"I-I wish there was another way." He brought his free hand to the protuberance welding their heads together. Their special bond. Their curse. "It's just not fair. Getting treated like monsters our whole life. And finding out fixing it means-"

"I'm sorry our life's been such a burden to you," Daniel said coarsely. "Sorry you need to take such extremes to be happy. But here's your chance. Dawes will be by soon. If he won't operate by choice, make him."

A violent sob hitched from Jonathan's throat. "I love you, brother."

"Just *do it*, Jon."

Jonathan squeezed Daniel's shoulder with his free hand. He raised the straight razor from the soapy dish to Daniel's throat, near the artery, and closed his eyes.

Forgive me, he prayed.

Dawes left Pinhead Rosie's tent, stepping into muck. The sky pissed on him for the third day straight, but he still whistled an off-key tune. Spudsville was a dreary little town, but Dawes decided he could settle here. It was hard to feel down when you'd been bitten by the love bug.

He never expected romance to exist in some dishwater pit like the Spudsville Tavern. But the second he'd set eyes on Marcie, well, his heart felt something other than deflation for the first time in years. It didn't seem right that such a fair-haired work of art would waste her time topping off the drinks of rosy-cheeked lushes. Dawes had waited for her to make her rounds before chatting her up. Tipped her big with money he shouldn't be spending. He even got a smile out of her. A goddamn genuine smile.

Were the feelings reciprocal? A simple glance in the mirror killed any such hope. Dawes himself could be confused for a sideshow act on appearance alone. The fairer sex usually high-tailed it at the sight of his onion complexion and hunchback slouch. His bulbous, pore-riddled nose slimed his moustache with snot, no matter the season. His hairline hadn't receded but retreated; a wispy crescent of course gray strands clung to the outskirts of his scalp.

But the circus was set to be in Spudsville for another few weeks. Enough time to lay on some serious charm. For the first time in years, ever since his practice folded, Dawes had a reason to wake up in the morning other than to give freaks physicals and prescriptions. Homely looks, lanky stature, and questionable career be damned, Marcie *would* fall for him.

He strolled through the muddy fairgrounds, whistling his gay tune. Two hours to show time and he'd nearly finished his rounds already. Just one more stop, and he could collect his daily pay from Barker Sullivan. Then it'll be off to the tavern to see his angel. And where some freaks like Lizard woman or Adult Baby would hold him up with complaints of dryscale or diaper rash, the Crabb twins would be a quick in-out checkup. They'd been sporting the cold shoulder after the awkward operation talk, Jonathan especially. Typical teenagers. Give 'em one harsh reality-check and you're the villain.

Dawes lifted the flap to the twin's tent and entered. The stench of blood hit him hard, overpowering the outside scent of rainwater and elephant shit. He dropped his exam bag and froze, powerless to do more than stare.

The twins had collapsed, clad only in stained under-shirts and briefs. From how they lay Dawes could not see faces, only the bulbous growth connecting their heads. Soapy water spilled across the tarp beneath them, leaking off the edges and into the earth. The foam atop the water had turned pink.

Blood was everywhere.

The gash carved into Daniel's neck spurted arterial fluids in a waning arc, painting a macabre abstract across the tent walls. The twin's undergarments were dyed deep sanguine. Jonathan's right arm cradled Daniel in a nurturing manner. He still clutched the razor.

Dawes turned from the tent's entrance and shouted to the gathering of workers and weirdoes outside.

"We got an emergency here! Freaks down! *Freaks down!*"

Nobody paid much attention, save for some clowns on a smoke break who simply rolled their eyes. Dawes grunted in frustration, snatched his exam bag, and stormed into the twins' tent.

It was clear, as he approached, that Daniel was fleeting. Statue-still, skin bone white, the life in his visible eye flickering out. Jonathan didn't look much better; suffering came in a package for twins like them. Jonathan side-eyed Dawes, and his mouth curled into a weak smile.

"So…Doc…" he croaked. "A-about that operation…"

THE FUNERAL TOOK PLACE AFTER THE SURGERY. JONATHAN was too critical to attend, which was well and good. Nobody wanted the sibling killer there anyway. He remained in a spare animal cage until the official trial could take place.

They placed Daniel's small body in the bearded lady's spare steamer trunk and buried him in the Spudsville Fairgrounds. Only Dawes and a handful of freaks bothered showing for the service. Not only did Dawes play the role of doctor and mortician, but he was drafted to be fucking gravedigger as well. Nobody trusted Pinhead Rosie with a shovel.

The trial was held before leaving Spudsville. Barker Sullivan acted as judge. A small jury was comprised of Geek-Boy, Lobster Hands, Lizard Woman and Bingus the Clown. Unlike Daniel's funeral, the trial drew a crowd. The bleachers inside the tent were packed with carnies, performers, and side-showers alike. Circus folk loved a good controversy. They all booed when the accused was presented in shackles.

The surgery had been successful, yet Jonathan's newfound normalcy was anything but. While his brother's corpse was removable, the bulbous growth connecting them was not. It jutted from his forehead like a bald, pink horn, giving his noggin an odd crescent shape. The lack of remorse in his eyes increased the crowd's hysterics.

The trial itself took no time. Dawes was called to the stand and testified what he saw in the tent that day. Jonathan made no arguments, replying to questions with simple shrugs. The jury convened, only to return ten minutes later. Bingus marched his oversized shoes over to Barker Sullivan and passed a note containing their verdict. Sullivan stood before the crowd and, in his best show-boating voice, made the announcement.

"In the case of Crabb vs. the Sullivan Circus Sideshow Community, the jury finds the defendant...*guilty.*"

The crowd erupted in cheers and admonishments. Sullivan continued once they calmed.

"Now this heinous crime *clearly* deserves the utmost punishment. In most cases, this would be a sentence of death."

"Hang the little fuck!" an incensed carnie yelled from the stands.

"But when we consider the life that Jonathan Crabb has lived, a life devoid of the slightest normality, it's hard not to empathize. The lad acted as he did in hopes of experiencing a living the rest of us take for granted. With this in mind, I cannot push for death upon Mr. Crabb."

Several boos ripped from the crowd.

"HOWEVER!" Sullivan continued. "It is clear to me that, for our safety, Mr. Crabb cannot remain with us. He may search for a normal life, but it must be alone. As of this moment, he is banished from the Sullivan Circus Sideshow Community. And with that, court is adjourned."

Barker Sullivan slammed his gavel amidst grumbles from the bloodthirsty. Carnies and circus folk filed from the circus tent, back to their repetitious lives. Pinhead Rosie squealed and spit at Jonathan as she passed.

The circus packed up for the next town, ready to leave ill circumstances behind in Spudsville. Dawes was the only one to wish Jonathan goodbye. The murderer dealt with his banishment like a champ, standing at the road leading to town with a smile on his face. His life was packed into a rucksack resting on his shoulders. He gripped a cane in each hand, awkwardly shifting his weigh to stand normal. He'd spent his life collaborating with his brother to get around. Walking alone was a hard task to learn.

"So what's next?" Dawes asked.

Jonathan fumbled with his canes. "Dunno. That's the exciting thing, I guess. I can go anywhere, do anything." His smile widened. "I'm by myself for the first time."

Loneliness ain't all it's cracked up to be, Dawes thought.

"You know what I really want to do?" Jonathan asked.

"Get a drink. I've never had one before. Daniel was against it. Evangelical upbringing. But now I can do what *I* want. You know a good place to drink, Dawes?"

"Spudsville Tavern's pretty good." Dawes thought about Marcie and felt a tinge of sadness. The murder, surgery and trial had put his blossoming love on the back-burner. He'd shrugged it off completely now.

An anxious look crossed Jonathan's face. "Hey, Dawes?"

"What?"

"Do…do you have any money I could have? Y'know, just to help me start off? I'll find a way to pay you back one day."

Dawes dug his wallet from his pants and fished out a few bills. He folded them and placed them in Jonathan's coat pocket.

"Thanks, Dawes."

Dawes nodded. "Well, I have to pack up. On to the next town." He turned to leave, stopped. "Take care of yourself, kid."

"Sure thing, Dawes." Jonathan began his long hobble on the path toward Spudsville. "The future's unwritten! My great adventure starts now!"

Dawes watched Jonathan head yonder until he disappeared. Though he tried denying it, part of him envied the kid.

1

Now

The town hadn't changed in the years Dawes had been gone. A perpetual gloom lingered over the skyline, and the rainfall turned the unpaved roads into mud pits. His shoes splashed through the muck as he trekked toward downtown Spudsville, passing decrepit shotgun houses. He greeted wary locals, who all walked as if the world had shit on them.

Dawes, on the other hand, felt giddy.

He'd stayed with the circus for seven more years, bouncing from the rust belt to the Northwest's evergreen sprawl. Every new fairground looked the exact same. Every time they packed up, Dawes considered running the other way and starting fresh. Yet the money was decent, and times were tough, so he stuck through.

But with time comes change.

The sideshow aspect of the circus folded after the Societally-Alternative Individual Rights and Management Act passed in congress. Most freaks either went back to their respective homes or took union-backed roles starring in upcoming horror movies. The circus lost its need for a full-time doctor. After Barker Sullivan offered him a job cleaning after the elephants, he decided it was time to make some life changes. Figuring out where to relocate wasn't hard; in the past years, Dawes had only felt fondness for a single place. With his final pay in pocket, he jumped the nearest train back to Spudsville. Back to Marcie's smile.

He arrived at the Spudsville Tavern shortly before happy hour, secured a seat at the bar, and ordered a whiskey from the ragged-looking barkeep. Dawes glanced around, hoping to catch Marcie clearing empty pints from the fold-out tables haphazardly placed across the floor. No luck. He nursed his drink, then another, before finally imploring the bartender about his mystery woman.

"Marcie?" the barkeep stopped pouring Dawes a fresh round. His face wrinkled as if trying to remember a long-forgotten friend.

Dawes grew impatient. "She used to work here? Blond hair, dynamite smile?"

The barkeep's eyes widened. "Ah, Marcie!" he exclaimed with a rotten-toothed grin. "She's dead."

Dawes' heart sank. "D-dead?"

The barkeep coughed a turgid load of phlegm onto the floor. "Dead. Suicide. How most Spudsvillians go. Somethin' 'bout the town's gloominess. Ain't a cheery place."

A lump formed in Dawes' throat. "That's horrible…"

The barkeep shrugged as he placed a fresh round in front of Dawes. "Felt worse for the cleanup crew. Girl took the classic *jump in front of a train* route. Hard to screw up that way. I saw the mess, and *phew*. Barely enough left of her to fill a bag."

"Dear god," Dawes murmured, his stomach queasy.

The barkeep shrugged again as he poured a beer for another patron.

"No god 'round these parts."

WITH NOWHERE TO GO, DAWES REMAINED AT THE BAR. HE drank whiskey until his vision swirled and his misery became a bleak joke. He'd either laugh about this situation one day or join Marcie on the train tracks.

His ninth shot slid down his gullet and something terrible swelled inside his gut. No food, too much whiskey. Dawes lurched from the bar, staggering across the floor toward the can.

The bile was halfway up his throat by the time Dawes reached the toilet. He dropped to his knees, ignoring the revolting wetness soaking his pants. A gut-load of liquor and stomach acid frothed from his mouth to the calcified porcelain bowl. Dawes gasped for air and continued puking until his stomach emptied. He collapsed to the dirty ground, sweaty, panting, and feeling lower than shit.

"Here for the money I owe ya?"

Struggling to sit, Dawes peered in the direction of the familiar voice. On a small stool in the corner sat someone he figured long gone. He must've been approaching his mid-twenties now, his boyish looks tainted by burst capillaries. The horn protuberating from his head remained hairless and pink. He wore cheap wrinkled dress clothes with suspenders and a name tag reading PISSER ATENDENT.

Jonathan Crabb smiled and stood, still supporting himself with two canes.

"Good seein' ya, Dawes. Damn good."

DAWES SWITCHED FROM WHISKEY TO WATER FOR THE remainder of Jonathan's shift. He was sober as a funeral by the time the young man finished up around ten or so. Jonathan gave the crusty barkeep, who he called Otis, the entirety of his tips in exchange for a bottle. The two men retired to Jonathan's place, a storage shed conveniently located behind the tavern.

Jonathan collapsed on a mildew-stained loveseat while Dawes stood. His head scraped the shack's ceiling.

"I didn't plan to stick around Spudsville for long," Jonathan said. He parked his socked feet atop his coffee table, beside a leather-bound tome with a long Latin title. "Just kinda happened. I built a hefty tab at the bar. They offered me odd jobs to pay it off. The drinking and the working balance each other out, I guess." He took a slug from the bottle and sighed. "It's more demeaning than sideshow work, though. People at least expect to see a freak in a circus tent. Speakin' of freaks, how's Pinhead Rosie doing?"

Dawes took the bottle from Jonathan and drank. "Rosie and Geek Boy went into law together after the sideshow folded. They're defending freak's rights. Turns out those two were smarter than anybody gave them credit for."

Jonathan chuckled. "Well, how 'bout that."

The two men passed the bottle, loosening up as inebriation settled.

"Did I ever tell you 'bout how Daniel and I could read each other's thoughts?"

Frowning, Dawes shook his head.

"Ever since we were kids, whatever he thought, I thought. He loved the connection. I hated it. I mean, it's hard enough having your brother literally attached to you 24/7. But not even getting the privacy of your own head-space? It's torture. And it's why I did the damn horrid thing. I spent my entire life craving a *single* moment of peace and quiet. You get that?"

Dawes nodded. Jonathan took a long drink. When he put down the bottle, his eyes had misted with tears.

"The real sad irony of it though? Now that I've had time to myself, gotten to see the other side a bit? It's too quiet in my head. I miss his voice. I miss it more than anything."

Silence again. They drank until the bottle was half-empty and Dawes' vision grew fuzzy. He studied Jonathan's face; the kid looked like his heart had been scraped out of his chest. Dawes knew the feeling.

"Can you do something for me, Dawes?" Jonathan asked, voice quivering. He pointed to the corner of his shack, toward a shovel propped upright against the wall.

Dawes looked toward the shovel, then back to Jonathan with an arched brow.

"I wanna…I wanna go back to the fairgrounds. Dig him up. I just need to see him once more. I—I didn't get to attend the funeral. Never got to say goodbye."

"You killed him. Is there a more intimate goodbye?"

A lone sob rose from Jonathan's throat. "Please, Dawes."

Dawes stared at the young man, mulling it over. Maybe it was his whiskey-lowered inhibitions or the disappointment crushing his spirits, but instead of refusing he sighed, shrugging.

"Fine, kid. I'll help you out."

THE SKY PISSED ON THEIR HEADS AS THEY MARCHED THROUGH slop. The muck threatened to suck Dawes' shoes off his feet. He carried the shovel in one hand, the diminishing bottle of spirits in the other. Jonathan rode him piggyback for time's sake.

It was past midnight once they reached the field. Dawes was drunk, tired. Not only did the simple prospect of manual labor feel crushing, but he had no fucking clue where he'd buried Daniel. The former fairground had become one giant mud pit the size of a football field, lacking any sort of landmark to jog his memory.

"I think we put him somewhere in the middle," he said. Once they reached the field's center, Jonathan dismounted and squatted in the muck. Dawes handed him the bottle, gripped the shovel, and started digging.

Two hours passed. Dawes finished a third hole, leading only to more earth. His muscles burned. Soaked clothing clung to his skinny frame. While the rain had subsided, a frigid bite in the air chilled his marrow. He dug harder, ignoring the exhaustion screaming at him to stop.

A foot into his fourth hole and the shovel's tip hit something hard.

"I—I found something!" he yelled to Jonathan, who'd fallen into a light sleep. The young man's eyes opened, and he sat straight, peering toward the hole.

A few more shovelfuls of dirt and Dawes could clearly make out the trunk lid. Its lower left corner had corroded inward, filling with earth. Dawes jabbed the shovelhead into the hole and pushed up, further disassembling the weak wood. Within minutes it was nothing more than broken pine and upholstery. The horrid smell emanating from the trunk didn't deter the men from inching toward the hole and peering in.

"There he is," Dawes said.

Time and elements had been unkind to Daniel Crabb. Gone were his funeral clothes, skin, and muscle. He was little more than bones speckled with the remaining sinew larvae had yet to finish.

"Brother," Jonathan croaked, voice quaking. He rested on hands and knees and craned his enormous head over the hole. "Dear, sweet brother." He turned away.

"Dawes…would you…would you remove him? For me?"

Dawes frowned. Jonathan looked to him with sad eyes.

"Please."

Dawes acquiesced with a grimace. He placed the shovel on the ground, sat in the mud, and slipped into the hole. He landed beside the trunk. The stink hit him like a wave. Holding his breath, he reached into the trunk and delicately lifted Daniel's remains. Bits of the boy snapped away and fell to the earth. Dawes placed the body beside the open grave before struggling from the hole.

Jonathan crawled over to Daniel's body, pausing for a moment before scooping his brother's remains into his arms.

"Dan," he whimpered. "I'm so sorry. I'm so, so sorry." He hugged the remains tight and started sobbing.

"What have I done?" he screamed. *"What the fuck was I thinking? I wish I could go back! I just wanna go back!"* His words morphed into incomprehensible wailing.

Dawes crawled out of the grave and sat up, his whole body caked in mud. The bottle of liquor sat just feet from him. He picked it up, uncapped it, and drank. He looked off into the horizon, where dawn was just breaking. A ripple of sunlight bled over the horizon like a wound. Dawes wondered if Spudsville would actually see a bright day. He imagined not.

Dawes took another drink from the bottle and listened to Jonathan wail.

2

———

Dawes considered getting his own place in Spudsville but opted instead to stay on Jonathan's moldy loveseat. He hoped it would motivate him to leave town sooner than later. He failed his attempts to hatch a quick escape plan and instead spent his first days drunk, staring at the ceiling, trying to ignore Daniel's withered remains propped on one side of Jonathan's mattress.

Jonathan was losing it. He still went to work at night, but spent his days fussing over the corpse. He'd never leave its side, constantly repositioning it in order to make Daniel appear more relaxed. He'd take the Latin book from the coffee table, flip to a random page, and read a passage to his brother. Then he'd stare intently, as if waiting for Daniel to respond. Once greeted with silence the sobbing fits would start anew, and he'd clutch the skeleton, wailing apologies. Stinking of whiskey, Dawes would watch these fits with the morbid interest of passing a brutal car wreck.

Three days passed before restlessness got the best of him, and he left Jonathan mid-tantrum. The midday gloom burnt like a thousand suns against his hungover brain. He hadn't looked in a mirror for days, knowing whatever stared back would be horrifying.

He made his way downtown, looking for Help Wanted signs. While escaping Spudsville was top priority, he cruelly lacked the funds to make that happen. But when he approached the storefronts, his heart sank. Most were abandoned, either boarded up or gutted. Detritus strew the streets in front of them. Somebody either sobbed or laughed from inside the dark, decrepit innards of an old diner.

He decided to try the tavern. It was full, as always, most of its downcast patrons drinking since morning. The air was thick with the smell of mildew and stale beer. Otis the barkeep smirked at the sight of him.

"Decided to stick around, huh?" he said while spit-shining pint glasses.

"Not for long," Dawes said, ignoring the doubtful look Otis cast him. "I was wondering if you knew of any available work."

"Work?" Otis squinted, as if the word was foreign. "Work's hard to come by in Spudsville. What kinda skills you got?"

"I was a doctor," Dawes said, omitting details such as his folding practice and under-the-table sideshow work.

Otis grunted. "We already got a doctor in town. We also got a vet who'll check ya up for half the price. Nope, no need for a doctor here." He placed a spit-shined glass on the shelf and started on another.

"Well how about you?" Dawes asked. "Need any extra help covering shifts?"

"Not unless you wanna get paid in liquor and bar nuts." Otis scowled and his whole face wrinkled like an old prune. He glanced across the bar floor. "If you're really desperate, talk to Eunice and Sal over there." He pointed to the bar's corner, to a table beside the broken jukebox. There sat a scowling, egg-shaped woman with one long caterpillar eyebrow, and a beanpole of a man whose moustache hid his mouth. "They're always looking for help at their pig farm. Ain't gonna be glamorous work, but it'll get you a paycheck."

Dawes approached the two, introduced himself, and explained his need. Eunice frowned when he explained his work experience.

"Pigs don't need no doctor," she said, her voice that of a talking cigarette. She pointed to her husband. "Sal here's doctor enough. Stitches 'em up after every fight."

Sal nodded and drank from his pint. Foam dripped from the bristles masking his lips.

"I'm not just looking for medical work," Dawes said. "Anything you've got, I can do."

"Got any references?" Eunice asked. "Anybody to vouch for you?"

"He knows Jonathan," Otis yelled from behind the bar. "Y'know, our piss boy?"

Eunice looked from Otis back to Dawes. "Would Jonathan recommend you?"

"I'd assume so," Dawes said. Considering all Dawes had done for him lately, grave digging and whatnot, he figured Jonathan owed him a lot.

Eunice considered, sipping off her ale. She eyed him up and down.

"Okay," she said finally. "We need someone to shovel up after the pigs. Safety suit's about your size, too."

Dawes was starting to think the world deemed him fit to only dig holes or shovel shit.

"Not as easy as it sounds," Eunice continued. "Lotta pigs, lotta shoveling. Mean bastards, too. Don't touch 'em. Don't look 'em in the eyes. Sal, show 'im what happens when ya look 'em in the eyes."

Sal raised his right hand and wiggled his two remaining fingers.

"So," Eunice said. "Ya in?"

Dawes' smarter half urged him to run from that bar, never looking back. His broke half justified that he'd probably done worse things for money before.

"I'm in," he said, unable to foster fake cheer.

He was wrong. He hadn't done *anything* worse for money.

Eunice and Sal raised fighting pigs; the fiercest in all of Spudsville and its neighboring counties. Once upon a time they provided the local diner with all necessary pork products. But after the economy went tits-up some years back and buying meat became a privilege, Eunice found the real riches in blood sports. Known as Spudsville's Savage Swinery, their farm was the best-kept secret of all reputable pig-men.

Dawes hoped the safety suit was an unnecessary precaution. Not so. The moment he crossed the pig pen's steel-enforced electroshock threshold, he was knocked into the mud by six hulking hogs. Squealing in fury, they pulled him across the ground like a ragdoll. If it weren't for the suit's heavy layers of padding, their massive jaws would've torn his limbs from his body.

"Just lay still!" Eunice yelled from beyond the pen. "They'll tire out, long as they don't taste blood."

It took ten minutes, but her words proved true. The pigs eventually grew bored of Dawes and scurried to the far sides of the pen. He struggled to stand, hampered by the suit's many layers. Sal threw a shovel over the threshold, which splashed in the mud feet from Dawes.

"Get shoveling," Eunice said.

The work was tiring and monotonous. Dawes filled a wheelbarrow with shit and wheeled it free of the pen. He dumped it in a field outside the farm, where Eunice and Sal grew corn and wheat to feed the pigs. Each time he returned to the pen, the hogs would mob him once more, forcing him back into the mud. He only moved seven barrels by the time his first six-hour shift ended, and his safety suit was tattered.

"We'll get you a new suit for tomorrow," Eunice said while handing Dawes a twenty-dollar bill for his efforts. "Good work today, Newbie. The pigs like ya."

Dawes knew he should pocket the money and go straight home, but after a day of swallowing pride and shoveling shit, he needed a drink. But as he stepped into the Spudsville Tavern, Otis curled his nose and shook his head.

"Sorry buddy, but I can't have you in hear smellin' like pig shit. It'll offend the other patrons."

"How's it any worse than mildew?" Dawes asked.

Otis shrugged. "Best I can do's sell you a bottle."

Irritated, Dawes acquiesced. As Otis handed him a fifth of scotch and ten dollars change, a thought crossed his mind.

"Hey Otis," he said. "Can you give me directions to the local graveyard?"

⚒———

It took time to find her amongst the rows of markers. More folk occupied the Spudsville cemetery than the actual town. Her headstone was nothing special, marked simply with the words *Marcie Klein*. Dawes sat on the wet ground before the stone and uncapped his bottle. He drank slow and cherished the burn.

"Would you have done it if you knew I was coming back for you?" he asked the stone before taking another drink. He poured a jigger onto the ground before him and sat in silence. Someone cried in the distance.

"Guess it's not all bad," he said. "You're here. I'm here. Doesn't look like either of us are leaving anytime soon." He let loose a half-hearted chuckle. "I guess, in the end, I got what I wanted."

Dawes took another drink.

3

O*ne more time,* Jonathan thought. *Then it's on to plan B.*

He studied the grimoire's pages from the corner of his bed, struggling to determine where he'd slipped up. While the archaic text was predominantly Latin, some words caught on his tongue and frayed his brain. Were they Hebrew? Sanskrit? Gibberish? He sounded out the passages for the umpteenth time, feeling more confident for this next go-around.

Standing from the bed, he limped carefully to the coffee table and set down the grimoire. He prayed to Daniel's skeleton situated on the loveseat. Dug into his pocket for his lighter and sparked a flame. Muttering protections, he lit the wicks of the candles lining the edges of the table: East, South, West, and North. He burnt wormwood until the smoke made his eyes water.

He looked down to the open pages and made another attempt at the incantation.

"*Colprizana, offina alta nuestra, fuara menut. Ego autem*

mortuus sum: In quo quaeris Daniel Crabb, et motrui sunt quaerite me."

He stopped at the sound of something stirring. Something like the wind blowing through trees, or a low, pained moan. When greeted with silence, he continued.

"Daniel Crabb spiritus Pomponius ducta defunctus est et nunc Veritam accedre ad hanc portam, et exaudi precam meam. Berald, beroald, Balbin, Gab, Gabor, Agaba! Surge, et ego invocabo te, et arguer!"

He stood, and as per the necromancy spell's instructions, approached Daniel's skeleton. He dug into his pocket and removed the straight razor, the same razor he opened Daniel's neck with those years ago. Jonathan extracted the blade, brought it to his palm, and carved a small line. He winced at the sting. A thin swell of blood rose from the broken skin. He smeared the red across Daniel's skull before returning to his spot by the coffee table. After extinguishing the candle's flames, he meditated.

Five minutes passed before he spoke.

"Daniel?"

Silence.

His heart raced. A lump formed in his throat.

"Daniel? Can you hear me?"

Nothing.

With a heaving heart he stood, flicking on the shack's lights. He faced his brother, who remained inanimate.

"God damnit," Jonathan murmured with a racking sob.

He'd known the rare likelihood of the grimoire actually solving his problems, but it had seemed worth a shot. Jonathan had found the tome in the Tavern's lost and found, left by a group of esoteric magicians who'd spent an evening swilling strong ales and failing to perform black spells. Since then, he'd tried his hardest to decipher its archaic text. Thanks to the sideshow's excellent home-schooling, he and Daniel had learned things the American public-school system couldn't fathom teaching. While the intensive course on dead languages seemed unnecessary at the time, it'd proven quite helpful in this situation.

But even top-notch translation can't make fraudulent spells useful.

The last of Jonathan's hope was crushed under the agonizing reality he'd hoped to avoid. Daniel was gone for good. No grimoire was going to bring life back to his remains. There were no second chances; Jonathan's past mistakes were unfixable, and he'd be forever alone.

Which mean it was time for plan B.

He considered opening his wrists with the straight razor and bleeding out right there. But why put Dawes through the trauma of finding that? Instead, Jonathan retrieved his canes from beside the bed. He hobbled to a closet in the far corner of his shed and opened it. Tools of all sizes and sharpness hung inside. Bypassing the garden sheers, chainsaw and hand axe, he instead grabbed a long, rusty chain coiled on the closet floor. He flung the chain over his shoulder and limped over to Dawes' luggage, where he found a long canvas coat.

Then came the tough part.

In what felt like hours, Jonathan managed to wrap Daniel's skeletal arms around his shoulders and stand. It appeared as if he were carrying a sleeping child piggy-back. He secured his brother to his waist with the chain and flung Dawes' coat over his shoulders. It hung past his feet, and with the addition of Daniel made him appear hunchbacked. But they'd look somewhat normal to the average passerby.

"Let's go, brother," he whispered to the skull resting on his shoulder and left the shed.

———

IT TOOK A GOOD TWO HOURS TO MARCH THROUGH THE HEART of Spudsville to the town's outskirts. The extra weight on Jonathan's back encumbered his trek. Nobody who passed noticed his bulky, awkward posture. They were too busy staring at their hole-ridden shoes.

He reached the tracks within another hour.

Jonathan had heard a story once about a Japanese forest where desperate people went to die. He supposed the Spudsville tracks were his region's forest. During his stay in the town, he'd personally known twelve people who'd thrown themselves in front of speeding trains. Heard of a good two dozen more who'd done the same. Nobody ever saw it coming, yet none were too surprised. Spudsville was just that kind of place.

Jonathan limbered over to the tracks, which pulsed with carrion stink. The rust of blood wouldn't fade from the American-made steel, despite the constant downpour. Scraps of gristle from past lives littered the earth between the tracks. Crows circled in the sky above. One landed on the twisted remains of a child crumpled beside the tracks and pecked bits of gore off his body.

He removed Dawes' coat, then unwrapped the chain from his waist.

He rested Daniel's body horizontally on the tracks before joining him, staring into empty eye sockets.

"This is it," he said, embracing his brother, "The end."

The wait felt like hours but may've been simple minutes. A mechanical chugging came from far ahead on the tracks. A billow of smog rose over a copse of dead trees, polluting the dreary skies. A horn squealed, shriller than a scream from the pits of hell.

Jonathan's exit came speeding toward him at 60 miles per hour.

As the train neared, his life flashed back in excruciatingly bleak detail. The good years with Daniel; the ones he took for granted. Then the miserable seven, after everything changed with the slash of a razor. He remembered waking, expecting Daniel to be there, *feeling* him there, only to find an empty spot on the bed. Cooking for two then eating alone. Finishing bottles alone, praying to choke on vomit while sleeping.

Jonathan figured himself dead for years, as dead as Daniel.

Now was the time to make it official.

He closed his eyes as the train closed distance, saying goodbye to this life, anticipating whatever came next.

"Off the tracks, Jon," someone said.

Despite the growing chug on the oncoming train, he heard the words clear as day inside his head. Jonathan opened his eyes, and gasped.

An ember glow emanated from Daniel's empty sockets.

"Come on Jon, *get us off the tracks*! You're no use as mush for the birds!"

Jonathan bolted up into a sitting position. The train grew closer before him, thirty feet, then twenty. The tracks beneath him rattled, growing hot. Jonathan fumbled his way off the steel, his heart rising to his throat.

The train bulleted forwards; fifteen feet, now ten. Gore from other lost souls streaked its front grill. Jonathan grabbed Daniel's skeleton, yanked it free from the tracks, and rolled away as the train sped by him. It stole the air from his lungs as it passed in a black blur.

Jonathan collapsed onto the ground, cradling Daniel in his arms. He stared up to the sky in disbelief, letting the rain splash onto his face.

"You're a real idiot," Daniel's voice echoed in Jonathan's skull. "You missed the part of the spell that said to be patient."

✦————

"So there's no heaven?"

"Or hell," Daniel said. "At least from my experience, that is. Who knows, maybe I was trapped in purgatory for all those years. Day in, day out, gray fog and silence. If you're telling me you felt lonely, you don't know half of it."

"Hasn't been a cakewalk for me, either."

Daniel scoffed. "Buyer beware, Jon."

They returned to town, Daniel once again chained to Jonathan's back and covered by the coat. He was still inanimate, nothing more than glowing eyes and a detached, telepathic voice.

Right now, that was enough.

They crossed thoughts all the way back to the shed. Rheumy-eyed locals looked at Jonathan sideways, thrown off by the wide smile splitting his face. They stepped back in alarm when he burst into random bouts of laughter. Joy was transgressive around these parts.

By the time they made it home, Jonathan's soul had filled. He threw off Dawes' coat in excitement when only a foot through the door and unwrapped the chain around his midsection. He placed Daniel on the loveseat and plopped next to him, resting his horn on the spot of Daniel's skull where they once connected.

"Dan," he said, trembling with emotional joy. "Can you ever forgive me?"

A pause from his brother, long enough for Jonathan to hear his heart beat.

"Absolutely not."

Jonathan's soul withered. He inched away from Daniel's skeleton and stared into his glowing orbs.

"But...I told you. I'm sorry."

"And I'm telling you that I don't accept. Apologizing isn't a fix-all, Jon."

Jonathan's joy kowtowed to an all-too familiar misery. "I...I've spent the past seven years torturing myself. Isn't that something?"

Daniel's eye sockets burnt an angrier red. "I'm glad it's been hard on you. It *should* be hard on you. But do you deserve a free pass for feeling human emotions the correct way? Hell no. Think about what you did, Jon. You bled your own damn brother out for selfish gain. And you have the gall to complain about feeling lonely, while I rotted in *purgatory*? Fuck you, *brother*."

Tears streaked Jonathan's face. "But you told me to do it!"

"No. I told you to do what you needed. I gave you a choice." He paused. "You made it."

They sat in silence, no thoughts passing between them. Jonathan stared out the window, eyes blurring, tears rivaling the rain outside. He regretted digging Daniel up. He regretted trying the spell. Most of all, he regretted rolling off of those tracks.

Daniel spoke after a spell, his voice still cold.

"But you can make things right."

Jonathan wiped snot with his sleeve and turned to his brother.

"It'll take some time, and it's not going to be easy. But with the right actions, we can start to mend. Do you want that, Jon?"

"More than anything," Jonathan whispered.

"Good. Now look at me. What do you think is wrong?"

Jonathan studied his brother.

"…You're a…" he fumbled his words.

"A what?"

"…a skeleton."

"That's right. I'm a skeleton. Your spell brought my spirit back, but without a proper vessel, I'm pretty much useless. I need you to fix this."

Jonathan frowned. "I don't…I don't get it. How?"

"Simple," Daniel said. "I need a new body. You want to make things right, Jon?"

The embers in Daniel's sockets glowed brighter than hellfire.

"Help me find one."

4

———

Dawes had worried about Jonathan's stability for days. Now he was certain the young man had lost it.

"You want me to do *what?*"

He sat on the loveseat, flabbergasted. Jonathan cradled Daniel's remains on the corner of the bed. A calm, expectant smile blessed his face.

"I want you to find him a body," he repeated.

Dawes leaned forward in his seat, elbows resting on knees, and stared at the floor. He could still smell pig shit —it clung to him like a perfume these days. After another long shift of shoveling waste and braving the maws of bloodthirsty hogs, all he'd wanted was to curl up with a bottle. Not deal with…whatever the hell this was.

"You know," Jonathan continued, "I didn't want to bring it up. But I *have* been letting you stay here rent free for the past week. I haven't asked for a cent of your shoveling money. Nor have I planned to. But maybe you owe me a favor instead?"

That's the little psycho's game, Dawes thought.

"Let me get this straight," he said, joints cracking as he stood from the loveseat. He paced around the small room, fidgeting with his snot-soaked moustache. "You want me to dig up another body, so your dead brother—who you claim is communicating with you via telepathy—can be something more than a skeleton."

God, even saying that sounded ludicrous.

Jonathan shifted uncomfortably, adjusting Daniel in his arms. "Well, you have some of it right." he paused, looking down to Daniel. His face shifted, and he glanced back to Dawes. "Dan says you might want to return to your seat."

"I'll stand," Dawes said flatly.

"Alright." Jonathan exhaled. "You can't just dig up a body. Anything in the graveyard will be either rotten beyond use or train mash. Freshness is critical. And getting something fresh means…well…"

Jonathan struggled to find the right words. No matter. Dawes put two and two together.

"You've lost it!" He snapped, storming over to his belongings. He grabbed shirts and dirty underwear off the floor and shoved them into his rucksack.

"What do you think you're doing?" Jonathan asked.

"Leaving." He stuffed everything he had into the bag and struggled with its zipper. "You've dove off the deep end if you think I'm going to stay here and kill for you."

Jonathan snorted. "Is it really worse than anything you've done before? Come on, Dawes, we both know why your practice closed."

Dawes' face blistered with rage and shame. "Nice try," he said, deflecting the low blow. Throwing his bag over his shoulders, he stomped towards the shack door. "Get professional help, Jon. Soon, before you hurt somebody again."

Jonathan waited until Dawes was halfway out the door until speaking again.

"He'll tell you how to bring her back."

Dawes halted in place.

"What?"

"Come back in."

"No," Dawes said, turning to face Jonathan. "Tell me right here."

Jonathan glanced back down to Daniel and nodded.

"Marcie," he said. "Help us out, and Dan will return the favor. He'll get you Marcie."

Something uneasy stirred in Dawes' chest. "How… how do you know her name?"

Jonathan nodded towards Daniel. "*He* knows."

Jonathan smiled as Dawes stepped back into the apartment. "Come on, Dawes. Take a seat. Let's talk."

Dawes' head swam with confusion as returned to the loveseat. "Everything you're saying…her, him…" Dumbfounded, he motioned to Daniel. "…they're dead. Long dead." He frowned. "What you're suggesting…it's impossible."

"Not with that," Jonathan said, pointing to the coffee table. To the leather-bound text surrounded by burnt candles. "With the right translation, anything is possible. Though you doubt me, it's brought him back." He rested his horn against Daniel's skull. "And with the right spell, you could at least talk to her. Finally try to woo her. Would you like that, Dawes?"

It couldn't be possible. Simply couldn't. Yet Dawes felt his head nodding up and down at the prospect.

Jonathan's smile widened. "And you understand what you have to do to make that possible."

Dawes stayed silent, contemplating everything. "Just any one body?"

Jonathan's smile faltered, and Dawes saw a slight panic in his eyes. "Well, not quite." He shifted on the side of the bed. "We want…things to be the way we were. We want you to attach us again. Can you do that?"

Dawes considered it and nodded. "I can try…"

The nervous look on Jonathan's face didn't fade. "Well, in order to do that, we'll need a similar body. Similar shape, and, well…size, to mine. Do you get what I mean, Dawes?"

Dawes' eyes moved from Jonathan's time-worn face to his skinny, small body.

It wasn't the body of a man, but of a…

…shit.

Dawes fought back the urge to scream.

5

H e drank from his flask outside the fence barricading Spudsville Elementary's playground from the world. The whiskey burnt on its way to his gut, a warm reprieve from the dreariness around him. He gripped the handle of the hand axe in one coat pocket. Felt for the pieces of candy in the other.

Dawes wondered if what he intended to do would be the worst sin he'd ever commit in this life. The answer was a resounding yes.

Jonathan was right. Dawes *had* killed before. But it was an accident; negligent and unethical, yet made with best intentions. Why waste precious time and excessive money waiting for a human organ, when he could do the same transplant with cow parts? It made sense on paper, and even worked at first. Three separate patients all left the operating table; one with a new spleen, two with a new liver. All lived happy lives free from excessive medical debt. Dawes' madness should have made him a medical genius.

If only the damn cow heart had taken.

Dawes hadn't hidden anything—the patient knew the risks. She was desperate, with little time left. If it hadn't been for that signed consent form, his punishment would have been much worse than a stripped license and a medical community blackballing. A life as an unlicensed sideshow doctor was better than one behind bars.

So yes, technically Dawes was a killer. But he accepted his mistakes.

This, on the other hand, helped nobody.

This would damn his soul forever.

He watched the children play, thinking they weren't much different than the vicious pigs he cleaned up after. They battled across the decimated field, mud slathering their bodies, rendering them androgynous. They fought not in organized herds but as an anarchic mass of gnashing jaws and scraping nails. An uneasy feeling settled in Dawes' stomach at the earsplitting sound of war woops. His task might be harder than he anticipated.

Dawes scoped a child disengaged from their warring peers, kneeling at the battlefield's sidelines. The kid appeared as androgynous as their classmates. They rotated between picking at their filthy, knotted hair and the mud beneath them. They plucked small insects from the mess and gingerly popped them into their mouth.

Dawes studied the ragged child. About Jonathan's size and build, the kid looked like they'd been raised to eat nothing but those damn bugs. Lacking the hostility of their peers, they seemed like a safe bet.

Dawes stepped forward, his face centimeters from the fence. He scanned the field for any adult presence and found nobody.

"Hey!" he called out, trying to gather the kid's attention while staying discreet. The kid remained inattentive, focusing on a nice-sized beetle submerged in muck.

Louder this time: "Hey, kid!"

The kid looked up, stared at him. Dawes cast a worried glance to the battling youngsters. None paid regard. His chest loosened and he returned to the child.

"Want something better than those bugs?" He removed a fistful of candy and held it out. The kid craned his neck, struggling to see. Dawes stuck his hand through a chink in the fence and spread his fingers, revealing a mound of stale ribbon candies atop his palm.

Squinting, the kid crawled on hands and knees to get a better view. They approached Dawes, interest competing with suspicion.

"Come on, take 'em," Dawes urged.

The kid brought their nose an inch away from Dawes' hand and sniffed the candy. The intrigue in their eyes grew at the drab, sweet scent. They took the top piece of Ribbon into their mouth and chewed, a smile spreading wide on their face.

"That's right," Dawes said, his grip tightening on the axe handle. "Eat up. There'll be more of that where we're going, if you just cross this—"

"*Stranger danger!*" yelled someone, her voice followed by the screech of a bullhorn. "*Retreat, children! Back to the bunker!*"

Wide eyed, the kid lurched away from Dawes. They turned tail and scampered back to the herd of children, who quit battle and scurried toward the school.

"Aw, for christ's sake!" Dawes yelled. "Come on, you little shit! Get back here!" He slid his hand back through the fence and tossed the ribbon candy into a puddle.

The bullhorn echoed throughout the schoolyard. A

squat figure barreled across the field, dead set on Dawes. The rim of a soldier's helmet rested above her furious eyes. Two wooden posts jutted from beneath the hem of her olive dress suit, their ends fitting into clunky combat boots. Despite the stiff prosthetics, she ran with the determination of a marathon sprinter. She held the bullhorn high over her head with one hand and clutched a rusted scabbard with the other.

Dawes was unsure whether to laugh or run.

The woman approached the opposite side of fence, her small button of a nose touching metal. Wiry gray hair puffed out beneath her helmet like brillo pads. Her round face was a plethora of deep scars, and Dawes noticed one of her eyes lolled loosely inside its socket. A fake, he suspected.

"Identification," she demanded in between pug breaths.

"Um, I don't have one, Ms..." he found a nametag on her lapel, surrounded by various pins determining rank. "Ms. Grace."

"That's *General* Grace," she corrected. "Now please state your name and purpose."

"Name's...Sullivan. I don't have any purpose," Dawes lied. "I was minding my own business when some kid called me over to ask a question. He...wanted to know the time."

General Grace snorted. "Nonsense. I saw you from over there." She pointed across the field. Dawes followed her gesture and wondered why he hadn't noticed the guard tower prior. "Now tell me," General Grace's glare sharpened, spinning her fake eye a full rotation. "What would an old man like you want with a young child? Are you a pervert?"

"No!" Dawes' face reddened, though he realized the accusation wasn't much worse than his real intent. "I just…I saw the kid eating bugs. I figured maybe he'd want—"

"*She.*"

"Okay—she'd want some real food. Is that so wrong?"

"Bugs are fine," General Grace said. "Full of protein. Helps them grow strong. Become better fighters. That way, they can replace the pigs."

Dawes frowned. "Wait, what?"

"Way those pigs fight, to the death? Their numbers are waning. Eunice and Sal deny it, but the whole sport'll be obsolete soon. No more hogfights means no more fun. No more fun means bloodier train tracks. But what we have here, on the playground?" General Grace smiled a wicked smile. "That's an unending supply of pure prepubescent fury. I have an entire league of fighters worth placing bets on, the way I've been training them."

"Shouldn't you be…I don't know…teaching them instead?"

"Pthhhhh," General Grace dismissed the question with a playful swing of her scabbard. "Teachers got laid off years ago. Parents still sent their kids here because hell, would you deal with them all day? Town needed someone to do *something* with them. So they hired me. And I don't teach. I train."

Dawes tried to find an answer but couldn't. He just stared dumbfounded at the strange lady before him.

General Grace hocked a goober into the muck. "Now listen, Sullivan, if that's even your real name." She crossed her arms over her chest and stared Dawes down with the menace of swarming hornets. "I'll let your intrusion pass. *This* time. But if I see you 'round these parts again, even looking at one of these kids, much less talking to them, or *feeding* them?" She abruptly sliced the air with her scabbard. "Things'll be much less pretty, my friend. Much. Less. Pretty. Got me?"

Dawes nodded.

"Good." she raised the bullhorn to Dawes' face and blew. "Now be gone, pervert!"

CRESTFALLEN, DAWES RETURNED TO THE SPUDSVILLE TAVERN. The air inside was heavy with the essence of bleach and puke. The clock read three and the place was packed. Dawes figured a few rounds might help him drum up a new plan.

Otis grimaced at the sight of Dawes.

"Told ya, I can't let ya stink up my bar, pal."

"But it's my day off," Dawes said.

"Sorry to say," Otis said, "but that hot pig trough smell? It's yours now, buddy, day off or not. Might wanna invest in some cologne." Otis blew his nose with his glass-cleaning rag. "Still want a bottle?"

Dawes sighed. "Please."

Otis left the bar to fetch a fifth. Dawes scanned the joint. Regulars slumped at their tables, some grumbling conversation, other staring into their smudged pint glasses.

Someone let out a distinct hearty laugh.

Dawes saw him immediately. Back turned, his shoulders rose and fell with each cackle. Unlike most Spudsvillians, his thick grey sweater was free from holes. His giant red puff of hair swayed as he smacked the table with his palm. Across from him sat Eunice and Sal, stone-faced as ever.

"And I told them…" he said in a thick eastern accent, struggling to catch his breath. "If I wanted to see a mime show, I'd go to that deaf school two counties over and sit in for free!" He cackled harder, threatening to upend the table with his slaps. Others around the bar looked at him with annoyance.

Dawes, on the other hand, saw him as a present dropped into his lap. Despite being built thicker than a tree trunk, the man struggled to see over the table. Dawes reckoned he was shorter than most of the children at the playground.

"Who's that?" Dawes asked when Otis returned with his bottle. Otis' face curled up like a squeezed lemon once setting eyes on the man.

"That cup of sunshine is Merrick Tibbs. Meanest pigman around." Otis spat. "His presence is a cavity in the tooth, if you ask me. He's too cheery, too confident. That type 'a attitude don't belong in Spudsville. He should take it back East where it belongs."

"Does he come around often?"

"Only when he's looking to buy a new beast from Eunice. Though I think he's staying longer this time. Grapevine says loony General Grace challenged Eunice to a showdown. Says her students are gonna tear the fat straight off Eunice's meanest hog. Ol' Tibbs, gambler he is, ain't gonna miss that fight. Reckon he'll be here at least through Friday." He grimaced. "Which means he'll be in here for too long."

Otis recomposed, and slid the fifth across the bar top to Dawes.

"Now time to hightail it, son. It's starting to smell like pig diaper in here."

⬥

DAWES TOPPED HIS FLASK WITH THE FIFTH AND LINGERED outside the bar. It didn't take long for him to make up his mind. After peeking through the tavern's windows and watching Merrick, he absolved himself of any guilt. Killing the man would feel much less sinful than any youngster.

Merrick remained in the bar with Eunice and Sal for hours, downing pints, cackling like he was at a funny picture. More than once he slapped the table hard enough to overturn Sal's pint. Merrick howled louder as the quiet man tried drying off his lap with thin napkins.

The sun had set by the time Merrick staggered from the bar, singing an off-key tune to himself. Dawes watched him from the shadows, feeling warm and confident from the liquor. Merrick turned left onto Main Street, sloshing through the mud towards the Grand Spudsville Inn. Dawes took foot once confident he was far enough behind to follow unnoticed.

They continued through blackened downtown streets, the lamplights extinguished and the stars above them blanketed by thick clouds. Not a soul stirred in the shuttered buildings surrounding them.

Dawes had to slow his pace considerably—Merrick's little legs only went so fast. The small man sang with the confidence of a Soprano and the skill of a mute.

"My old pig can't fight like she used to, can't fight like she used to, can't fight like she used to..." his voice cracked on every vowel and he swayed with his words, like even the slightest

wind would topple him. *"My old pig can't fight like she used to, so I'll eat bacon in the morn."* He cackled again, freeing phlegm from his lungs. He stopped walking, as did Dawes, who ducked by the ruins of an old pharmacy to watch.

"How about it, Spudsville?" Merrick yelled. He puffed his chest out, as if issuing a challenge, and stared down the vacant buildings. "You got the balls to handle Big Merrick? Think you can even handle Big Merrick's balls?" He fell silent, waiting for a response. "No?" he said spitefully. "I didn't think so."

Grumbling something about dumb sonsabitches, Merrick fumbled with his belt buckle. He wavered like a cattail in the breeze, nearly toppling into the muck.

"I got a present for you, PUDSville," another hearty laugh as he pulled his trousers to his ankles. "Incoming package, courtesy of true greatness."

A grunt was followed by a splatter. Any lasting apprehensions over killing the man faded as Dawes watched Merrick empty his bowels on the muddy downtown street. He took a final pull from his flask before pocketing it and removing his hand axe. Then he stepped, quiet as possible, into the street.

Another grunt, another splash. The sharpness of Merrick's waste stabbed Dawes' nostrils. Every step forward brought a swell of nervousness and excitement. Dawes closed the distance between them. Twenty feet became fifteen feet, then ten. He raised the hand axe over his head, anticipating swinging it into Merrick's skull.

At six feet away the mud swallowed his shoe, emitting a loud squelch. Dawes froze, his blood icing over. Merrick tensed at the sound of intrusion. He turned his head, peering at Dawes with a wild eye.

"What's this?" He demanded, voice seething. "Some lowlife tryin'a sneak one on Big Merrick?"

Dawes took a nervous step back, foot pulling free from his submerged shoe. He quickly returned the axe to his pocket while fishing for an excuse.

Merrick swiveled around, his boot narrowly missing his own excrement. "You got balls, piss-ant." His hand cupped below his waist. "But tell me. Are they bigger than these balls?"

Though skewed in the darkness, Merrick's handful *did* appear rather impressive.

Merrick stepped forward. "Come on, creep," he said. "Show me what you got." His voice became a rabid snarl. "Come on, pervert. Show big Merrick your balls."

Dawes' assertion segued into fear. He backpedaled further, stumbling over apologies, paying no mind to the cold mud soaking his old sock.

Run the fuck away, his brain commanded.

Merrick let out an animalistic shout before Dawes' body could respond. The little man charged, head lowered, bulleting faster than Dawes could ever anticipate. Dawes barely had the chance to yell before Merrick's skull sank into his gut, vacuuming the breath from his lungs. They both toppled to the ground, splashing in the mud. Dawes tried crawling away, but Merrick jumped on top of him, straddling him. The first fist crashing into his jaw helped him forget the weight of the testicles resting on his gut.

"Nobody fucks with Big Merrick!" the little man yelled, unleashing a flurry of blows to Dawes' face. Each punch landed like a sledgehammer to cinder. Knuckles split his lips and loosened teeth. His nose pulped, spraying hot blood and snot, and his vision danced between static and fireworks. He tried going for his pocket, for the hand axe. Merrick's knee pinched his side, obstructing his reach. Panicked, Dawes blindly groped the ground around him, hoping for a large rock. No luck. Out of options, he dug a handful of mud free from the earth. In one swift motion, he jettisoned the filth into Merrick's face.

"Fuckstick!" Merrick bellowed, ending his blows to scrape earth from his eyes. Taking advantage of the refrain, Dawes drove a palm into Merrick's throat. The attack worked better than expected; Merrick emitted a wet choking sound and faltered, wrapping hands around his neck. Dawes rolled, violently shifting his weight to the left, casting the little man off of him. Overcome with the audacity of freedom, Dawes turned onto his stomach and scrambled, trying to crawl to his feet.

A heavy weight crashed onto his back, planting him face-down into the mud.

"*You dog dick!*" Merrick managed, voice little more than a croak. He gripped Dawes by his wiry tufts of hair and forced his head further into the earth. Dawes struggled, releasing his remaining breath. Mud filled his mouth. A terrified worm squirmed in the mess, tickling his uvula, teasing his reflex.

For the first time in his life, Dawes understood the fear of drowning.

His consciousness spun outward as Merrick maintained hold of his head. Struggling only depleted his last reserves of energy. He toed the line of a warm, black void. A soft, sultry voice called on him to jump to the other side. He couldn't be sure, but he thought it was Marcie.

"*Nobody…fucks…with   Big…Merrick…*"   said   a competing voice above him.

With little options remaining, Dawes surrendered, diving into the void.

———

HE AWOKE ON HIS BACK, STARING AT A SKY TRANSITIONING TO a lighter shade of gray. Rain pissed down on his face, breaking apart the mud caking his swollen features. Every single inch of him ached. He smelled shit and wondered if Merrick had dragged him through his waste. That or he was finally noticing his own pig trough stench. Competing with feces was the odor of death.

Vultures circled above his head, waiting for him to die off so they could eat. He swore he could hear them groan when he sat up, wincing through the pain. He looked to his left and right. The sodden earth around him was flat, peppered with dead copses of trees in the distance. Beneath him were train tracks, crusted with human remains varying in age and freshness. His mind raced, trying to remember how he'd gotten here. Realized Merrick had wanted to frame Dawes' death to look like the average Spudsville suicide.

Well played, Big Merrick, he thought.

He patted his coat pockets, feeling for his flask. Gone. But Merrick *had* left the hand axe, so at least that was something. Groaning, Dawes laid back down on the tracks and stared up at the drab sky.

He wondered what he'd say to Jonathan when he returned to the hut. Would he feel shame? Was it possible to even feel shame anymore? Dawes had hit rock bottom before and didn't think it was possible to dig deeper. But laying on train tracks, battered and covered in a little man's shit? That seemed like a new low.

He considered staying there and letting the train fulfill Merrick's intent. Becoming a mile-wide streak of gristle and bone would be a mercy. Sayonara, Spudsville. Thanks for nothing.

But the cold became unbearable the longer he stayed on the tracks. His stomach growled for food and whiskey. After another hour without a train, Dawes' impatience overruled his will to die.

He stood up and headed back to town with his head hung low.

6

Jonathan went about his usual schedule, trying not to stress. He'd hoped Dawes would return with good news by the time he'd left for work. No such luck. He tried shrugging off the idea of Dawes ditching town. Had the request been too much? Was Dawes counties away by now?

"Why leave to someone what you can do yourself?" Daniel asked as Jonathan mopped grit off the floor of the tavern's stall. "I mean, you're more than capable. I'm a shining example of that."

Jonathan ignored the edge in Daniel's voice and focused on his work. He'd known taking his brother with him was a risk. Not only did the weight of Daniel chained to his back encumber his abilities, but it made him look downright strange. Even with Dawes' coat draped over them, the two together was a sight to behold. Fortunately, nobody seemed to pay notice. Jonathan resigned to the fact that he was invisible to most.

He emptied his mop bucket and returned to his attendant station. Daniel pressed him further as he restocked paper towels and complementary ribbon candy.

"How do we know Dawes will even find the right body? I can't speak to him. He doesn't know *my* preferences."

"Does it matter?" Jonathan asked, tasting the hand sanitizers for freshness. "Look at what you have now. Won't anything be better than that?"

He could feel Daniel's eyes glow a deep sanguine under the coat. "Why should I settle, Jon? I didn't exactly lose my old body by choice. Is it wrong to think you owe me?"

Jonathan said nothing. Shameful as it may be, two days in with his brother and his patience was already tested. Daniel wasn't about to make things easy. Given the circumstances, Jonathan couldn't blame him. He'd just hoped the reunion would be a bit cheerier.

The bathroom door opened and a rather large, oafish Spudsvillian stumbled in. Jonathan sat straight and faked a smile as the man waddled over to the stall, drained himself, and made for the exit without washing his hands. Jonathan still offered a paper towel. The oaf ignored the courtesy and dug his unwashed mitt into the bowl of ribbon candy, taking a generous handful before leaving. The door slammed shut behind him.

Daniel snorted. "Some career you have," he said.

His shift finished and he found an empty bar stool. Otis readied him a well shot with an ale chaser.

"Getting drunk, huh?" Daniel said. "I guess that's one

way to spend the time. Instead of, you know, finding me a body?"

Jonathan downed the shot as soon as Otis set it in front of him. He knocked it back without shuddering, savoring the burn.

"See you've had a lot of practice at that," said Daniel.

Jonathan resisted the urge to respond with venom. He sipped off his ale and flagged Otis for another shot. He watched clientele with downturned faces filter in and out of the bar. Listened to the rain continue with its consistent downpour outside. Somewhere in the distance, a familiar voice shouted. General Grace, he guessed, leading her child fighters on a night drill.

The clock neared ten when the door opened and a strange character stepped in. Half-hearted snippets of conversation ceased as patrons looked away from their dirty glasses.

"What the fuck?" Otis spat as the figure approached the bar.

He was slim, tall, dressed in nylons. Face painted bone-white, a black diamond beneath one eye, spade under the other. A beret sat atop his head, off which hung a gold tassel. Lipstick a deep shade of merlot accentuated his smiling mouth.

The strange man gave a small bow to Otis and pulled something invisible from behind him. With an exaggerated gesture, he peeled back the pedals of an imaginary flower, gave it a quick sniff, and placed it in an empty pint glass. He laughed in silence and clapped his white-gloved hands together.

Otis looked at the mime with inconvenience. "Whaddya want?"

The man cupped his left hand together and placed it on

the bar. With his right, he pretended to pour a jigger of spirits. He knocked back the invisible shot then pretended to stumble, eyes crossing with drunkenness.

Otis gave him a deadpan stare. The smile sloughed off the man's face and he relaxed, shrinking an inch or two in the process. He stopped sucking in his gut, which stretched his nylons to capacity.

"Bourbon," he demanded in a guttural growl. "A bottle. Cheap."

Otis nodded, turning away to fetch the order. The sound of the man's voice rang familiar in Jonathan's head. His mind backtracked to a time filled with calliope music and the musk of elephant shit.

"Bingus?"

The man turned, staring Jonathan down. His eyes widened in surprise.

"Crabb?" a disbelieving smile spread across Bingus' face. "Well cover me in cowhide and milk me dry. Little Jonny Crabb, in the flesh." His smile thinned. "I didn't recognize you all by your lonesome."

"Yep, just me now," Jonathan said, rubbing his horn. He awkwardly shifted Daniel's weight on his back. "Living the life of an only child."

"I forgot we left you in this hole," Bingus said, then spared Otis an apologetic glance across the counter. Otis shrugged and resumed his task of watering down the liquor bottles. "I figured you would've escaped by now."

"It's not that bad," Jonathan lied. "Dawes came back as well. Lives with me now."

Bingus snorted. "*Dawes* came back? Well, that's a shocker. After he quit the circus, I assumed he'd return to the black-market cow organ game."

"Not that I know of." Jonathan frowned. "Hey, what

are you doing here, anyway? Is the circus stopping back through?"

A smug grin crossed Bingus' face. "I'm not with the circus anymore. I gave up the clown life years ago."

"Oh," Jonathan said. He eyed Bingus' getup. "Well, what about…"

"For Chrissakes." Bingus scowled. "I'm a *mime*, not a clown. Don't you simpletons know the difference?"

Jonathan shook his head. Otis shook his head. Bingus seethed.

"Uncultured swine," he muttered, shooting down his bourbon and signaling for a refill. "I quit the circus and joined with *Cirque Fantastique*. It's not a circus. It's high-brow. Art. And not only that, but they treat their performers with dignity. I have benefits. I get fed more than peanuts and cotton candy. It's steps above the big shoe, tiny car, pie-in-the-face life Barker Sullivan forced me into." Unbearable smugness returned to his face. "At least there's one success story coming from that shithole."

Unable to produce a response, Jonathan sipped his beer. He remembered a different Bingus—a goofy, kind-hearted fellow, hiding his morose behind face paint. Clearly the mime life had gotten to his head.

Bingus continued. "We needed to fill a few days of our tour, and it turns out Spudsville-" his face curled in disgust just saying the name "-was the only stop with *any* sort of population between cities. We have a few nights booked at the old stadium just outside town. And I have to say…" He glanced at the tavern's weathered patrons. "This dreary place looks like it needs the magic only *Cirque Fantastique* can offer."

There was a loud knock on the tavern window. Otis turned his head and yelped, jumping.

"What the shit is that thing?"

Jonathan peered to the window. A small face painted a ghoulish white pressed against the glass. A black heart was sketched under one eye, and a club beneath the other. Its eyes peered about the room hungrily. It smiled as its gaze met Bingus.

Bingus smiled back to the little creature and waved. "Don't mind him. That's just my boy, Antonio."

"*His boy*," Daniel whispered inside Jonathan's skull.

"There're rules against leaving your child unleashed outside establishments here," Otis said. "Might wander off. Or more likely, General Grace will take it home with her to train."

"I best be off anyway," Bingus said. "We have to prepare for our show. And I'm sure Antonio's getting cold out there in the rain." Bingus pulled the collar of his nylon leotard down and reached in, feeling about. He pulled out gold coins and set them on the counter for Otis. He then turned to Jonathan. "And for you…" He dug back into his leotard, pulled out two slips, and set them on the counter. "Here're free tickets, for you and Dawes. Come see some *real* entertainment."

"Thanks," Jonathan said, still staring at Antonio's painted face.

Bingus turned once more to Otis. "And would *you* like some tickets, sir?"

Otis spat. "If it ain't pig fighting, I ain't interested."

Bingus sniffed. "Fair enough." He stood from the bar and started toward the door, pretending to grasp onto an invisible rope, struggling as if scaling a vertical surface. Step by pained step, he reached the doorway and stepped out into the chilly Spudsville night.

Jonathan and Daniel followed Bingus out of the tavern,

watching from a cautious distance as he removed a leash from his nylons and latched it onto a collar around Antonio's neck. As Jonathan watched Antonio follow at Bingus' heel, he could feel Daniel practically quiver with joy.

"Perfect size, perfect shape…" Daniel's voice salivated in Jonathan's head. "That Boy, Jon…he's the one."

— ⚬ ———

"Let me get this straight," Dawes said, standing up from the loveseat. He scratched at his face and winced at pain's sharp retort. "You want me to kill the child of someone who knows us—actually knows us—and sew his corpse onto your body to allegedly serve as a vessel for your dead brother."

Jonathan paused, then nodded.

"And you don't see how that could go terribly wrong?"

Jonathan sighed. "Believe me. I know it might. But it's not up to me." He nodded over his shoulder, to the skeleton still tied to his back.

Dawes stared into Daniel's dark, vacant eye sockets. He shook his head. "This keeps getting worse and worse." He stood by the window and squinted out at the downpour. His reflection stared back weakly. Hours after his beating, his face was already a landscape of bruised lumps. His bulbous nose swelled to twice its normal size, occupying half the area of his face. His every breath was a tea kettle whistle. His wispy brillo-hair spiked in mud-muddled licks, gracing him with the look of a mangy lion.

"Just…why Bingus? He's a gentle clown."

"*Was*," Jonathan said. "You didn't see the way he acted, talking down to us. The mime life's gotten to his head. It's rotted him out. Think of it this way…" Jonathan stood from the bed and shifted his feet, trying to support Daniel's weight on his back. "...by taking his kid, we're doing the world a...a cosmic service, if you will. Garbage people raise garbage children, who grow up to be garbage adults themselves. You'll be saving society from having to deal with another asshole, all while giving a kind soul a second shot at life." He reached over his shoulder and pet Daniel's skull. "You'll be a good Samaritan, Dawes."

Dawes frowned, bearing the pain doing so caused. "I just...I dunno. No. This has gone far enough." He spun around in a fury, rage scaling his ribcage. "This hunt of yours is screwy, and it's only brought me pain. I've been called a pervert, *twice*. A scary little man beat me to the brink of death, dragged me through mud, and left me to die on train tracks. His balls touched my chest, Jon. His *balls*."

He was yelling now, spittle flying from his split lips on every pronounced vowel. His fury skewed Jonathan's face into a look of discomfort.

"Look Dawes," he said, bracing his hands before him in defense. "I—I know things've been shaky. But it's all part of a process! This first difficult step is through. We've found the perfect body. Now we just have to obtain it. Remember what we promised you. Do this and she's all yours."

Dawes scowled. "Why should I even believe you, Jon?" He dug into his coat pocket, removed the hand axe, and tossed it to Jonathan's feet. "I'm done," he said, gathering his things and walking toward the door. "If you want this so bad, do it yourself."

Jonathan broke into a jumble of pleas and retorts, ranging from *please don't leave* to *you've done worse, you murdering bastard.* Dawes fought the urge to punch Jonathan in the face and made his way out the door.

"She's still alone, you know," a familiar voice echoed inside his head.

Dawes froze. He slowly turned, the hair on his neck standing upright. A tingling fear crept up his spine as he faced the impossible.

"She laid on those tracks hoping to end that loneliness," Daniel said, his eyes aglow like embers. "But there was no escaping it. Purgatory, where she floats now? That's the loneliest place of all. Lonelier than you can ever imagine, Dawes. And that's where she'll remain, unless you do the right thing."

Dawes felt drugged. He floated back into the room, unable to control his feet, and returned to the loveseat.

"Don't you want to free her, Dawes?" Daniel said, voice thick with coercion. "Don't you want to give her the love she needed to live? And receive love too, in turn?"

Dawes nodded. He swore he saw a grin spread on Daniel's skeletal mouth.

"Do this for me, and I'll make it all possible. You'll never be alone again."

Dawes stared into Daniel's smoldering sockets. "Never again?"

"Never."

He sank into the loveseat, considering the offer. It all seemed too good to be true, but strangely less fantastical coming from Daniel's corpse. Dawes took a long moment to consider it all before speaking.

"So Bingus went bad, huh?"

"Real bad," Jonathan said, smiling. He lifted the hand axe from the ground and carried it over to Dawes, who took it in his hands. "Rudest mime there ever was."

7

———

Jonathan picked items from the tavern's lost and found box for clever disguises. A driver's cap and dark shades for him, a cowboy hat, bolo tie and matching sunglasses for Dawes. Jonathan drew a goatee around his mouth with a half-pencil of eyeliner. He kept Daniel strapped to his back and covered with Dawes' coat. Dawes' battered face added to his own disguise.

Together they trudged through town, past the refuse of downtown Spudsville. Anxiety chewed at Dawes' gut. He was lightheaded after not eating all day. He'd tried swallowing down oatmeal, but it just sat in his mouth until he spat it back into the bowl. His stomach felt full of rocks.

Ahead, two figures nailed flyers to light posts beside the road. One tall, lanky man, and a squat redhead with a mean build. Dawes' face flushed with panic. Sal and Merrick turned and started walking their direction, engaged in a one-sided conversation on Merrick's behalf. Dawes tipped the rim of his cowboy hat low, masking his face. He slouched and slowed his walk, faking a limp to alter his appearance further. Beside him, Jonathan stared at Dawes with confusion.

Sal and Merrick walked by without paying attention to the three. Merrick cackled at his own joke and slugged Sal in the arm, damn near knocking him into the road. Merrick laughed harder as Sal regained his footing. Sal hung his head a bit lower as the two walked off.

Dawes managed a glance at the sign the duo hung before the rain reduced it to pulp. *Fight of the Century*, it read in bold letters. Underneath sat two grainy photos; an unkempt child baring its teeth, hands curled into claws, and a wild hog with a murderous glint in its eye.

Blood will stain the mud when General Grace's little lunatics take on Eunice's one and only BOSS HOG. Who will be the victor; The Terrifying Tots or the Sadistic Swine? Come find out this Friday, inside the old Spudsville Diner! Five bucks a head. No food or drinks.

"I still don't get this town," Jonathan said as they continued onward toward the mime show.

THE SUN HAD DESCENDED BY THE TIME THEY REACHED THE Old Spudsville Stadium, about two miles out of town. The thing was less a stadium and more of an extra-large pig pen covered by a tarp. Barker Sullivan's circus had looked more appealing to the eye.

They took shelter in a gathering of dead trees and watched a small group of Spudsvillians make their way into the tent.

"Should we go ahead and enter?" Dawes asked.

Jonathan shook his head. "Why would we actually go in? Watching the show would make us complicit. And let's face it, Dawes. Even with our disguises, we stick out."

"Yeah," Dawes said. "But I wouldn't mind seeing the show, free tickets and all."

"No show," Daniel confirmed in Dawes' mind.

The clock struck six. A glow emitted inside the pen. The familiar jingle of calliope filled the air, and through the thin layer of tarp, Dawes watched six silhouettes stand before a sparse audience. They started what appeared to be a haphazard tumbling act, mixed with sight gags involving invisible props. Occasionally an audience member would clap, likely unsure what else to do.

"This is what mimes do?" Dawes asked.

"I guess." Jonathan said.

Dawes wondered how in the hell Bingus could afford such a good life.

The show ended after an hour. The calliope abruptly ceased and the handful of audience members bumbled free of the pen, wandering aimlessly back to town.

Fifteen minutes later a second group left the "stadium" in matching black nylon and white face paint. All six stood roughly the same height, lanky save for the beer guts stretching their outfits to capacity. A leash accreted from the hand of the front-standing mime. Attached to the leash's end was a boy in a similar getup.

Bingus and Antonio, Dawes guessed.

The caravan of seven walked in the opposite direction of Spudsville, along a winding road. One walking beside Bingus carried a lit lantern. They pretended to walk against a nonexistent blustery wind, as if facing the threat of being blown away. Dawes and Jonathan waited until the group made distance before creeping behind them unnoticed.

The pursuit lasted another hour, halting several times when the mimes found themselves caught behind invisible glass thresholds which required comical teamwork to maneuver across. Watching the unshapely exhibitionists tumble through the mud seemed like a better show to Dawes than the one locals paid to see.

After what felt like a days' worth of travel and an exercise in Dawes' patience, the mime troupe arrived at two small buildings. An inn and a tavern, both dilapidated. They were the only structures in sight along the flat, lonely landscape. A sign above the bar read *The Soggy Boot*. A handful of weary women in scant clothes smoked cigarettes beside the door.

The mimes made their way single file toward the tavern. Some mingled with the women outside, fawning and handing out imaginary roses, receiving nothing but unenthused smiles until removing real-life money from their nylons. Three of the mimes waltzed toward the inn with the women, a jubilant spring in their steps.

Bingus walked his son to hitching posts mounted outside *The Soggy Boot*. He secured the leash around the middle post, tying it in a slipknot for extra hold. He patted the boy on the head, then reached into his nylons and pulled out an apple. The boy gnawed greedily at the treat as the remaining mimes filtered into the pub.

Dawes and Jonathan stood in the distance for what felt like millennia, expecting Bingus to come from the bar to check on his son. Time passed with no sign of the elder mime.

"Better get moving, huh?" Daniel pressured.

Dawes swallowed. His heartbeat pounded in his ears. "So...how should I do this, again?"

Jonathan sighed and shook his head. Daniel spoke with reproach.

"How many times do we have to go over this? Lure him over here. Keep him intact—I want this body in the best condition. Only use the axe if need be. Don't make a scene. Clear?"

Dawes nodded. "Crystal," he said.

"You have the bait?"

Dawes reached into his pocket and removed the ribbon candy.

"Good. Now's the time, Dawes."

The distance to *The Soggy Boot* didn't take long to cover, but it felt like a voyage. Dawes gripped the axe handle in his coat pocket, waiting for the pub doors to burst open and drunken mimes to filter out. A nervous tension in his chest spread to his gut and shoulders.

A lone dull streetlight cast a yellow glow around Antonio. The child pushed his apple core around the mud with fading interest, glancing up in alarm when Dawes was within ten feet. He bristled, stepping back, parting lips and exposing jagged yellow teeth.

"It's okay, son," Dawes said, slowing his pace. He inched toward the boy with caution, holding the ribbon candy out before him on the flat of his hand. "Just thought you might be hungry. Want a treat?"

Hesitant interest replaced the defense in the child's eyes. The rigidity in his shoulders decreased as he made one small step toward Dawes.

"Good," Dawes said, smiling. "Every nice boy likes ribbon candy. Come, take it."

The distance between the two closed. The boy grew more comfortable as Dawes approached. He craned his head toward the candy and sniffed.

"Keep going…" Daniel's voice echoed in Dawes' head. "Nearly there…"

Dawes raised his candied hand to the boy's mouth, and with the other reached to the latch on the collar around his neck.

"Eat up."

The child opened his mouth, leaned in, and chomped his jagged teeth down on Dawes' pointer and middle fingers.

Dawes' brain short-circuited with pain and alarm. He screamed in shock and tried drawing his hand back, launching the ribbon candy from his palm. Growling, Antonio clamped his jaw like a bear trap, shaking his head like an angry dog tearing at roadkill. Dawes' vision blurred. He fell to his knees as the child's teeth scraped bone. He dug into his pocket for his hand axe.

"*Don't!*" Daniel yelled.

But it was too late. High on terror and adrenaline, Dawes pulled the axe from his pocket, yielded it over his head, and swung. The child finally released Dawes' fingers as the blade sank into the left side of his face. He emitted a sputtering gag before collapsing to the ground, convulsing.

Dawes slumped onto his ass, staring in shock at the remains of his ruined fingers. The boy's animal teeth had severed the digits at the second knuckle, leaving them dangling by meaty strands. Blood pulsed around the ridges of exposed bone, cascading down his forearm. His head grew light and his body heavy as his consciousness started a steady retreat.

"NO!" Someone yelled behind him. Feet pummeled the mud; whether ten feet or one hundred feet away, Dawes neither knew nor cared. He simply stared at his fingers and their skin threads, his vision growing spotty.

Jonathan slapped him across the face, bringing him back a bit.

"Get up, Dawes, get up." Another slap pushed him an inch closer to reality. "Out from the open. Out from the streetlight."

Daniel's incense drowned out the panic in his brother's voice. "You idiot! You fucking imbecile! What part of 'keep him intact' was so difficult? You ruined *everything.*"

Dawes' response came out mush. He wiggled his hand and watched in a stupor as his severed fingers danced like marionettes.

"For Christ's sake." Jonathan grabbed Dawes' fingers with a frustrated grunt. He yanked, tearing the skin connecting to Dawes' hand, then shoved the digits into his pocket. Jonathan grabbed Dawes' shoulders and shook.

"Come back. COME. BACK."

He rattled the last of Dawes' shock away. The sharp pain of amputation arrived first, then the horror. A terrified moan left Dawes' mouth once his eyes shifted from his nubs to the boy's body. He leaned off to the side and vomited in the mud.

"Get up, Dawes," Jonathan urged, grabbing Dawes' coat and yanking. "We have to get that boy out of the light and wrap your hand. You're losing too much blood."

Dawes managed his way to his feet. The earth around him wobbled, threatening to topple him once more. Jonathan set one cane down and tried taking some of Dawes' weight. They staggered clumsily toward the boy. Dawes leaned against the hitching post as Jonathan unhooked the leash from the boy's collar.

"Grab him."

Dawes complied, threading his working hand into the boy's nylon and dragging him. He swore when the nylon ripped in his fingers.

"Try the handle."

Dawes grabbed the axe handle. His stomach lurched once more, and he fought back the taste of hot bile. He yanked, expecting the axe bifurcating the left hemisphere of the boy's face to pull free. It held. Jonathan supported Dawes once more, and the two awkwardly shuffled toward the side of the pub. The dead boy dragged behind them, leaving a trail of carnage in the muck.

Dawes stumbled behind an overflowing dumpster, wheezing, fighting for consciousness. Jonathan tore off the coat draped over himself and Daniel and dug into his pocket. He removed the straight razor and hacked at the seams of the coat sleeve until the fabric tore free. Jonathan wrapped the sleeve tight around Dawes' mangled hand, securing it with the bolo tie.

"That'll have to do for now," Jonathan said. "We'll need to cauterize those stumps soon though." He glanced to the body on the ground and whistled between his teeth. "God, Dawes. What a mess. This really cocks up our plans, you know? Can't have Daniel walking around with a split—"

A creak rose from the tavern's entrance. The bar door, opening and closing. Feet squelched into mud, and a flint struck steel. There was a pause, then a low gasp.

"Antonio?" said a familiar craggy voice.

Jonathan cursed under his breath.

"Antoooooonio," Bingus called again, voice rising to a playful pitch. He whistled, clapped his hands. "Here, son! Come to Bingus!" Worry seeped into his tone.

Both men tried keeping still and quiet. Dawes eyed the trail the boy's body left in the mud and prayed Bingus wouldn't notice.

The sound of the first footfall smashed his hope.

Jonathan sprang into action beside him, trying to shove Antonio's little body into the crevice between the dumpster and the earth. He stopped once Bingus rounded the corner of the bar. Jonathan tried striking a natural pose against the dumpster, hoping his awkward frame would conceal the dead body sticking out.

Bingus stopped at the sight of them. He clutched Dawes' cowboy hat in his hands, which was stained in blood and filth. Dawes hadn't even felt it fall from his head.

"You two?" His face skewed with confusion. He shifted a thin cigarette from one side of his mouth to the other. "What are you doing out here? We chose this place to be *free* of the locals. Were you even at the show?"

"Uhhhh…yeah…" Dawes managed.

"Christ, Dawes," Bingus said, stepping forward. "Time has not been kind, my friend. Your face…your…" he looked to the makeshift bandage containing Dawes' hand, already soaked red. "What the cold hell happened there? What'd…"

His eyes shifted from Dawes to Jonathan, then Jonathan to Daniel. He took an anxious puff of cigarette. His sights set on the figure shoved haphazardly beneath the dumpster and he froze. The cowboy hat slipped from his hands and met the ground below.

"What the fuck is that," he demanded, voice trembling.

Jonathan straightened and stepped forward. "Now Bingus, listen, whatever you think you're seeing right now, believe me…there's a rational explanation. We're just—"

Bingus kicked, his foot branching the distance between himself and Jonathan. His slippered heel caught Jonathan in the gut, launching him backward. Jonathan slammed into the side of the dumpster, ricocheted off, and landed face-down in the muck.

Bingus took a reproachful drag of tobacco and stormed over to the dumpster. Kneeling, he grabbed the figure beneath by its little left arm. He dragged the small body out from its hiding spot, into the open. His mouth gaped, dropping the smoke into the mud, as he peered at the figure's face.

"Ant...Antonio..." He struggled with his words. "What—no, wake up, son, wake up. You're going to be okay, we'll just...just remove this..." He grabbed the axe handle and tried pulling to no success. Dawes had really planted the blade deep.

Bingus' voice split with a low, pained sob. The sound encumbered Dawes with a heavier guilt than he'd ever experienced. He was unsure whether to run or console the mime.

He thought harder and decided fleeing was undoubtedly the best choice.

Dawes leaned on his good hand and tried rising to his feet. The world spun—he *had* lost a lot of blood. Still, he managed to stand, and took the first stumble away from the building.

From next to the dumpster, Jonathan moaned and tried standing. The sound caught Bingus' attention, who whipped around, landing on his feet with tiger-like grace.

"I don't fucking think so!" he yelled. He swung a foot into Jonathan's face, sending the little man back to the ground. Without missing a beat, he charged Dawes, closing the distance between them in a blink. Dawes hadn't the chance to scream before Bingus slammed into his back, thrusting him face-first into mud. Bingus grabbed onto Dawes' ankles and dragged him back to the dumpster. Dawes clawed at the ground to no success.

"Murderer!" Bingus screamed, flipping Dawes onto his back. "Predator! Child-killer! *Pervert!*"

I'm not a fucking pervert, Dawes tried yelling. Bingus forced his mouth open before he could speak, and with a free hand, shoved in a pile of mud. Bingus slammed Dawes' jaw closed and clamped a palm over his lips.

"You fucked with the wrong mime," Bingus said, sneering. He reached under the collar of his nylon and removed a small ivory object. He pressed a button and cold steel extruded with a loud *snick*. He raised the switchblade to Dawes' face, tracing a teasing line from his lips to his swollen nose, rising until reaching his forehead.

"Let's let the whole world know what you are, pervert."

Dawes screamed. Bingus dug until steel scraped bone, carving a line up Dawes' forehead, stopping above his scalp. Hot pain erupted from the incision, scrambling Dawes' vision. The blade turned a sharp left and started a new line intersecting the first. A warped smile spread across Bingus' mouth as he carved. His tears splashed Dawes' face.

"After this, I pull out your insides," he said finishing up the first letter, starting upon the next. Dawes felt the familiar haze of waning consciousness. His lights flickered, threatening to extinguish. Death seemed warm and peaceful compared to this.

Then Bingus screamed.

The carving stopped. The blade slipped from Bingus' hand, hitting the mud with a dense splat. The mime fell with it, landing on the ground and thrashing. Dawes wiped blood from his eyes and sat up.

Jonathan grimaced while gripping Bingus' ankle and working his straight razor through the mime's Achilles tendon. Bingus howled and tried kicking Jonathan away with no luck.

"Get the knife!" Jonathan yelled through split lips.

Dawes scrambled up, every inch of him aching. He dug through the mud with his good hand, pausing to wipe gore from his eyes with his sleeve. He found the blade's end first, slicing open his palm. Dawes winced then tried again, this time finding the hilt.

Bingus shook Jonathan free. Grasping his ankle to stop the bleeding, the mime limped toward Dawes with a fire in his eyes. Dawes flipped the mime onto his back and knelt over him.

"Forgive me," he said, and dug the switchblade into his opponent's chest. Bingus let loose a pained wail. Dawes pulled the blade free, allowing hot blood to geyser upward. Bingus gasped, slapping his hand atop the wound, but Dawes stabbed once more, this time closer to the heart, then again, and again, and *again*, until there was nothing more than a ragged cavity. The mime stopped screaming, stopped moving completely.

Both Dawes and Jonathan collapsed to the ground, fighting to catch breath.

"That..." Dawes struggled for words in between wheezes. "That didn't...didn't go so well."

Jonathan nodded in agreement. He rolled onto his side, crawled over to Bingus' body, and dug through the mime's nylons. He removed a small brass object and struck at its flint until drawing flame.

"Take off your bandage," he said, holding his straight razor's blade above the ignition. "Let's stop the bleeding."

8

The rain paused on their trek back to the shack—a small mercy, but a mercy nonetheless. Dawes draped Bingus' arm over his shoulder, supporting him like an intoxicated friend. He draped the ruined cowboy hat over the mime's face as a disguise. Jonathan threw one of his walking canes in the *Soggy Boot*'s trash and dragged Antonio behind him by the axe handle. Fortunately, nobody passed them on the way to Spudsville.

They returned to the shack in the early hours of the morning. The sun still slept behind the horizon. Dawes dropped Bingus' body on the floor and collapsed onto the loveseat. Every inch of him ached. The scorch around his missing fingers already smelled of infection. He saw his reflection in the window, grimacing at the message Bingus carved into his forehead. A *P* and half of an *E*.

Jonathan left Antonio's body next to his father's and limped over to the supply closet. He opened the door and started digging.

"What're you doing now?" Dawes asked.

"Daniel says there's still work to do."

Dawes realized he hadn't heard the other Crabb's voice in some time. "Why hasn't he said anything to me?"

"Silent treatment," Jonathan said. He grunted as he grabbed something from the closet floor and turned, struggling to carry it out.

A chainsaw.

"Whoa, whoa, whoa," Dawes said, sitting upright on the loveseat. "What the hell are you doing with that?"

Jonathan set the chainsaw on the ground by the bodies. "What *you're* going to do is make it up to Daniel. Look at these." He motioned to the bodies, first to Antonio. "We have a good body here. Right shape, right size. Head's ruined, though. Now over here," he pointed toward Bingus. "We have a head in pretty good condition. A little older than we wanted, definitely some wear and tear, but passable, overall. Body's all wrong, though, and there's no fixing that hole in his chest." Jonathan moved the cane to his other hand and shifted weight, rattling Daniel's bones in the process. "So in the end, we've got two working parts in an otherwise damaged system; two parts that could pair together nicely. Get what I'm saying, Dawes?"

Dawes looked from Antonio, to Bingus, to the chainsaw. He wanted to protest but was too damn tired. Staring at the bodies, he sighed.

"You're trying to damn me to hell, aren't you?" he said to Daniel.

Daniel said nothing in return.

***

THEY DISPOSED OF THE EXTRAS ONCE THE DEED WAS DONE. This time Dawes was the one with a body chained to his back. His overcoat bulged, stretching to support the added width of Bingus' headless corpse. The vital fluids sloshing from the mime's neck quickly turned cold in the morning air, adding to Dawes' discomfort. Beside him, Jonathan carried Antonio's head in a sack. They'd left Daniel at home. The skeletal Crabb was still subjecting Dawes to the silent treatment.

Dawn was only just starting to tease the horizon when they arrived at Eunice and Sal's farm. They walked soft-footed across the property, keeping an eye out for traps. If caught trespassing, Dawes wondered if Eunice would go easy on him, being an employee and all. He imagined not.

The hogs were already restless once they approached the fence. The beasts hurried across the mud and stopped at the other side of the chicken wire, sniffing, snorting and growling. Dawes wondered if they already smelled Bingus' blood.

He unchained Bingus from his back, allowing the corpse to fall into the mud. Stepped into the supply shack by the pen and changed into his hog-proof suit. Found the key to the pen hanging by the shack's doorway. He took the sack from Jonathan, removing Antonio's head before unlocking the pen's gate.

"Here we go," he said, stepping in.

The hogs went wild at the sight of him, as per usual. They scampered forward, gnashing mandibles, ready to feast. Dawes chucked Antonio's head across the pen while he still had time. It sailed high then descended into the mud, landing face-down with a wet *thwack*. The swine halted at the sound, at the *smell*. They turned, appetites piqued, and raced toward their new snack. The six hogs fought each other over the head, nipping at each other while tearing Antonio's skin and muscle clean off his face.

Powerful jaws reduced his skull to splinters and his brain to paste.

As the beasts feasted on the head, Dawes dragged their next course into the pen. Once Bingus' body was past the threshold he turned and left, locking the gate behind him. By the time he changed from the hog-proof suit, Bingus was little more than entrails and slop.

Pale-faced, Jonathan stared at the feasting hogs.

"What horrible beasts," he said.

Dawes nodded. He sleeved away snot from his moustache and watched the last of Bingus disappear. "Well, that's it, I guess."

BACK AT THE SHACK, HE GOT TO WORK ON ATTACHING Bingus' head to his son's body. He tried cleaning the makeup off the mime's face to no success. Dawes couldn't help but applaud the determination it took to tattoo mime makeup on oneself.

The actual process of conjoining head and body became a chore. Jonathan knew there was leather string in the tavern's lost and found, but the bar was closed for another few hours. They had to act fast—the pieces were already starting to smell sharp. Dawes dug around the supply closet for anything useful and came across a small tackle box, shoved deep into the closet's rear. He opened it and smiled. Inside were a variety of hooks and fishing wire. Not exactly quality stitching thread, but it would suffice.

Dawes laid the body and head next to each other on the floor, so their stumps touched. Then he secured wire to the end of a bait hook and brought it to the ragged end of the head's neck. He pushed the hook's point into flesh and forced it through the other side, conjoining it with the body. He pulled the wire taut and proceeded onward.

The task was tough. Dawes was long removed from his surgeon days, and back then he'd had full use of both hands. His missing fingers made him clumsy, yet he soldiered through. It took two hours to stitch the head to the body. The result was less than stellar—the spacing between stitches varied from millimeters to a full inch, tight in spots, bunchy in others. Opaque fluid leaked from the excision, forming a rank puddle on the shack floor. The head tilted at an awkward angle, like it was perpetually staring left.

Despite the flaws of the job, Daniel couldn't be happier.

"It's…it's perfect…" he said, breaking his silent treatment toward Dawes. "It's more beautiful than I imagined."

Jonathan smiled wide at his brother's approval and stared at the body in admiration. Dawes didn't get it, though he supposed any body was better than a skeleton.

"What's next?" he asked Daniel.

Dawes could hear the glee in the boy's disembodied voice.

"Reunite us."

9

———————

I f attaching the head to the body had been a struggle, this was unfathomable. But low and behold, Dawes accomplished what was asked of him.

He had to commend Jonathan for being a trooper. Without anesthetic and unwilling to risk the thinning of blood via alcohol, the only option for a painless surgery was to knock the boy out. Jonathan chose to stay awake for the horrid process, feeling everything. Dawes didn't know if he had an ounce of the boy's dedication.

Jonathan lay on his left side. Dawes positioned the body on its right so the two stared into each other's eyes, close enough so that Jonathan's horn rested on the body's scalp. He sterilized the fishing hook with Bingus' lighter, attached more wire, and began sewing.

Jonathan held his sobs in, even once Dawes started pushing the hook in deep. He trembled as his blood collected beneath him, soaking the knees of Dawes' pants as he worked. Every once and a while Daniel would offer soothing encouragement, a *there, there, brother,* or *you're so strong, Jon.*

Dawes believed it.

After the first hour Jonathan went completely still, and Dawes realized he'd passed out from the pain. Jonathan's newfound stillness made the work easier to finish. Like the conjoining of Bingus' head to Antonio's body, the job looked shoddy. But when Dawes lifted Jonathan and shook, the wire held him together with the corpse. Mission accomplished.

Daniel guided Dawes through the next steps. Dawes paint a circle around the two with Jonathan's blood. Moving the candles from the table to the circle, he placed one on each end before lighting their fuses. He found the wormwood in the supply closet and burnt it, overpowering the smell of rot with strong incense. He scraped the last of Jonathan's blood from the bowl and painted a small star on his forehead, then the corpse's, then Daniel's skeleton. Daniel directed him to the appropriate passage inside the grimoire and helped him with pronunciations.

"Kumeth Agripheth sanda Jonathan es Daniel Crabb," Dawes recited, scrolling a page whose title roughly translated as *The Spell of Resurrecting Possession*. "Spiritus Exhaum Verdati, Convuset—"

"Convu*seth*," Daniel corrected.

"Convu*seth*, Dernaga, Crabbs conjoina."

As he read on, the temperature in the apartment increased. Beads of sweat formed at the ridge of Dawes' scalp and descended his swollen face. A low moan rose from somewhere in the shack from neither Jonathan, Daniel, nor the corpse. Dawes ignored the sound and the subsequent fear kneading his gut.

"Kargis veniscotha ressurectus, Van hasda Crabb twins, Satanis peridontious..."

A loud crash rang above his head. Chunks of the

shack's ceiling tore away, sucking into a black funnel cloud staring down at the ritual. Dawes screamed, expecting the vortex to pull him into an abyss. Miraculously, his feet remained planted on the ground.

"Finish!" Daniel yelled. Dawes stared back to the page and managed the last line in the weakest of voices.

"Klandus ciggureth, Vandau! Daniel es Jonathan Crabb, connectus eternitus!"

The moan became a deafening scream. Dawes clamped hands over his ears, dropping the book. Something flashed in the corner of his eye. He turned, gasped.

Daniel rose from the loveseat, steadily ascending into the air. The skeleton's empty eye sockets burnt a blinding red, pouring out snakes of electric energy which surrounded him, encapsulating him in a sharp static field. Dawes' wispy hairs stood on end as he watched the Crabb rise higher, *higher*, reaching the vortex then disappearing inside. Once he was gone, everything stopped; the ceiling reformed and the screams ceased. The candles snuffed out all at once, and Dawes found himself standing alone in heavy silence.

Jonathan stirred on the ground before him. His eyes fluttered open, and he let out a pained mumble.

"Daniel?"

The corpse attached to him lay still. Heaviness overtook Dawes' heart—all that work for nothing.

With a shaky hand, Jonathan nudged the corpse. It remained lifeless. Jonathan released a sigh rattled with defeat.

"So much for that," he said.

The corpse's eyes opened.

Jonathan and Dawes both cried out. The body blinked slowly; Bingus' former eyes burnt a fiery red. He raised his left hand and curled the fingers, watching each digit move. A smile spread across his painted lips. He took a deep breath and a sharp whistle emanated from a loose stitching on his neck.

"I'm back," Daniel said with a guttural wheeze.

Jonathan let out a happy chirp. Dawes froze in disbelief.

"I can't believe it worked," he muttered.

"Brother, I—I'm so happy…" Jonathan wiped away joyful tears. "We did it…we…we're whole again…"

"That's right," said Daniel. "Together forever, Jon."

They stood. Jonathan struggled more than Daniel. Not surprising, given the blood loss. Daniel hooked his arms under Jonathan's armpits and supported his brother's weight. Together they walked as they used to—sidestepping carefully, relying on their peripherals to see their surroundings. They headed to the bed and sat upright on its corner.

"Walking will take a while to relearn," Daniel said. Jonathan laughed through the tears.

"I guess in the years spent walking by myself, I unlearned *our* way." His voice was weaker than Dawes expected.

"Jon," Dawes said. "Do you need water? You're looking awful pale."

Jonathan started to nod but Daniel cut him off.

"He's fine. We're fine. Isn't that right, Jon?"

"Fine," said Jon. Dawes felt a buzzing concern. The boy looked awful.

Daniel, on the other hand, looked ready to run a marathon—despite the wonky stitches and the subtle rot.

"Listen," Daniel said, peeking at Dawes from the corner of his glowing eye. "I think it's important for us to get some brotherly time in. Think you can allow that, at least for a few hours? Tonight's the big hog fight. Maybe check that out for a while."

"What about my end of the deal?"

"Oh…" his face scrunched in remembrance. "Right. Marcie. Okay, get me the grimoire and a pen."

Dawes obeyed. Daniel rested the old text on his and Jonathan's laps and flipped through pages.

"Here it is," he said, landing on a spell. "*Profectus Amore Resurrectum.* Resurrection of a Lost Love." He flipped over the sheet he'd transcribed for Dawes earlier and wrote down the new spell. "Bring one candle and the wormwood. Draw some blood of your own and drip it into the soil over her grave. Say these words, bring her soul back. Try and make a connection."

"That's it?"

Daniel nodded. "Easy."

Jonathan's eyes sagged. "I don't feel too hot," he said, shivering.

Daniel shooed at Dawes with his hand. "Now be off. Please, leave us be."

Dawes stared at Jonathan, unable to shake his concern. But the urgent look in Daniel's eye told him it was time to leave. He slipped the candle, the wormwood, and the transcribed sheet into his coat pocket and started toward the door.

"Dawes…" Jonathan said behind him. Daniel whispered something cross to his brother.

Despite his better judgment, Dawes left the shack to meet his lost love.

HE WAS SURPRISED TO SEE THE WHOLE DAY ALREADY PASSED. The sun retreated past the horizon, and a cold rain fell hard.

As Dawes passed the tavern, he noticed its lights were off. It couldn't be later than 9—far too early for closure. Shouting echoed in the distance, intensifying as Dawes continued toward downtown.

Main Street, normally empty, swarmed with what Dawes estimated to be half of Spudsville's populace. They formed a sloppy circle spanning from one side of dilapidated storefronts to the other. Some held butane lanterns, providing illumination. All swayed with gleeful inebriation, too sloshed to notice the rainwater overflowing their pints. Under the cover of an umbrella, Otis filled empty glasses from a sputtering keg. The ales looked mostly foam but the patrons didn't care.

"Eat those little fucks alive!" A crusty tavern regular shouted into the circle. Some cheered. Others turned and offered the man chastising glares. Dawes crept to the side of the circle and pushed his way through spectators.

The circle's middle was roped off, forming the crudest of rings. Chaos reigned inside. On one side of the ring six little bodies stood in attack stances. A seventh lay in the mud, little more than bone and gristle. On the other side stood a giant pig, its height surpassing all the swine in Eunice's pen.

Remembering the signs he'd seen Merrick hanging the other day, he guessed this must be Boss Hog.

Merrick himself stood at the edge of the ring, white-knuckling the rope and hopping in excitement. The rain matted his frizzy hair to his head in wet strands.

"Gnaw those little shits to nothing!" Merrick shouted. "Turn their balls into breakfast!"

On the opposite side of the ring stood General Grace, who stared at the battle with a look of determined focus. She adjusted her battle helmet and barked commands.

"Attack formation! Surround the beast from all sides! Go for its underside with your teeth! Semper Fi, never surrender!"

General Grace's little soldiers formed a crescent around Boss Hog and charged, aiming for the swine's bulbous belly. But once the children were in striking distance Boss Hog whipped its massive body around, striking down the soldiers approaching on the left, then on the right. Small bodies landed hard in the mud and desperately scrambled upward. Boss Hog stormed toward an androgynous-looking soldier, opened its gaping mouth, and clamped down. The sound of child-sized bones crunching between enormous jaws rang audible over the spectator's collective cringe. Boss Hog pulled away, taking the child's arm and flinging it into the crowd. Two Spudsvillians fought over the limb like a souvenir. Boss Hog then tore the child's throat free and stomped a herculean hoof onto their ribcage, caving it in.

Merrick cackled. Beside him, Eunice smirked. General Grace bellowed in fury. Her remaining troops charged Boss Hog once more, their little hands and mouths doing minimal damage to the giant beast. Another child went down as Dawes pushed his way through the crowds, turning his head to avoid the slaughter.

The raucous sounds of battle echoed in the distance once Dawes reached the cemetery. He walked the path as he best remembered it. Striking a flame on Bingus' lighter offered him sparse illumination. He covered the fire with his free hand to keep the rain from extinguishing it and studied the names upon the gravestones.

His heart lit up when he found the name *Marcie Klein*.

He remembered Daniel's instructions and troubleshot. He took off his coat and kneeled, then draped one end of the coat on the headstone, the other on his shoulders. He placed the candle on the wet grass and lit its fuse, then burnt the wormwood. The fragrant smoke burnt Dawes' lungs and eyes. He coughed and tried ignoring the discomfort. He remembered the next step—*draw some blood of your own*. Felt his pant pockets, then the coat above his head.

Fuck.

He'd forgotten a blade.

His mind raced with innovations. He picked at the mouth of the lighter, trying to bend the steel into points sharp enough to open flesh. They scratched him no better than a cat's claws.

Droplets of water soaked through the thin fabric of the coat above him, landing on his forehead, threatening to extinguish the candle. He panicked as his window of time started shutting.

He removed the gauze covering the stumps of his ruined fingers. He curled his nose at the stink of infection rising from the cooked flesh beneath. Without proper medical attention, he'd lose more of the hand.

What he had to do now certainly wouldn't help.

Dawes pictured a juicy, plump steak resting before him and bit into the healing skin of his ruined hand.

His stomach rioted as he worked through burnt scar tissue and into a pocket of pus beneath. The pain was excruciating, the taste offensive. He bit and chewed until the copper tang of free-flowing blood met his lips. Sanguine rivulets leaked from the fresh punctures decorating his stumps, running down his forearm. Dawes quaked with pain but smiled. He hung his hand over Marcie's grave and let the blood spill onto the grass.

Then he removed the transcribed spell sheet from his pocket, and by the dull flicker of the candle, started to read.

10

———

Everything felt wrong. Jonathan waited for the weakness to subside and the room to cease spinning. If it weren't for the fishing wire connecting him to his brother, he'd slide off the bed and onto the floor.

Brother.

It didn't seem like the right word for this new Daniel.

He stared into glowing red eyes which once belonged to Bingus. A smile dredged with cruelty and viciousness spread across the former mime's face. The Daniel he'd once known was incapable of expressing such malice.

After what seemed like ages of silence, Jonathan finally spoke. His voice came out frailer than he expected.

"So…what's next for us?"

"What do you mean, *brother?*" A taunting edge in Daniel's raspy voice cut Jonathan like a knife. The chilling smile remained.

"I mean…we…we can move on, away from…away from Spudsville. Can't work at the tavern like…this."

Even forming thoughts seemed tough. His gut churned with anxiety, yet he continued.

"And this…this shack. We don't need this shack." He tried to raise his arm and signal about. He couldn't lift it past his shoulder. "We can find…something…better…"

Daniel said nothing. That grin of his turned Jonathan's blood into ice water.

"D-Dan?"

"How do you feel, Jon?" The smile widened. What big, jagged teeth Bingus had.

"I don't…I…I feel…"

"Weak?"

Jonathan paused. "Y-yes…"

"Then it's working." Daniel stood from the bed. Jonathan lifted with him, his feet scraping against the ground. Daniel walked, not in their awkward cooperative shamble, but as a strong, capable individual carrying his brother like dead weight. Jonathan tried talking, but his words failed him.

"I, for one, feel great," Daniel said. "Better than I ever have. Better than you ever will. I feel like I can move mountains, Jon. Like I have the strength of armies. Why do you think that is?"

Jonathan scraped for an answer and came up empty. Daniel filled in the blank.

"I'm taking back what was taken from me, *brother*. Seems fair, doesn't it? What was drained from me all those years ago can be taken back now."

"But I…I brought…"

Daniel sneered. "What, you brought me back? You think giving me a second life as a patchwork corpse clears *your* crime? Pitiful, Jon. Murder requires the ultimate price to pay. A *life for a life*, brother."

Jonathan panicked. Where was Dawes? He knew he saw a look of concern on his old friend's face. Maybe he was coming back, to burst through that door any second and—

Daniel read Jonathan's thoughts and snorted. "You think Dawes can help you now? Please, Jon. He's off searching for unrequited love. And believe me, when he summons what's in store for him, he won't be making it back here."

"…what…?"

Daniel blurted a cold staccato laugh. "You think I'm going to help him? The one who assisted in my death? Who, instead of saving me, cut me away from you and left my body to decompose in some hole? Believe me, Jon—his fate is mapped out, as is yours. Retribution's a whore, *brother.*"

Tears welled in Jonathan's eyes. "You…you're not my brother…"

"I am, Jon. I am and so much more." Daniel paced around the room. He wiped a descending tear from Jonathan's cheek and licked it off his thumb. "When I said I went to purgatory? Not quite true. I went somewhere else. Somewhere hotter. Surprising, right? Me, the evangelist, cast into a place where torture made years pass like millennia. The suffering broke my altruism. My resentment and hatred grew to a level impressing the Dark One himself. He struck me a deal. He'd bring me back, give me the chance for revenge. All I had to do was find someone dumb enough to spread his message." That horrible smile. "Case and point, Dawes."

Jonathan's mind swirled. "But…*I* brought you back."

"Do you really think those magicians left the grimoire at the tavern on accident? All part of the plan, Jon. Agents of Satan, doing his bidding."

It all seemed so unbelievable. But who was Jonathan to

know? His thoughts were growing harder to link together as his energy further drained.

"W-what are you doing to me?"

Daniel smirked. "Simple. I'm draining you of your soul. Once it's mine and you're nothing but a corpse, I'll pass it on to the Dark One. Yours, matched with the bountiful amount which Dawes will unwittingly hand over, will be my ticket to eternal life. And judging by how I'm feeling, and how you're looking," Daniel paused to chuckle, "we're almost there."

Jonathan was positive he'd never felt worse. Betrayed. Beliefs shattered. Life rapidly draining from his body. He thought of Dawes, in the graveyard, about to receive the surprise of his life.

And it was all Jonathan's fault. Every single bit of it.

Daniel kept talking, but his words lost clarity. Something inside Jonathan rivaled the dread, sadness, and waning energy. It was something bitter and burning. A fire ignited by betrayal. He'd *tried* to correct course, damn it. He'd admitted his mistakes and attempted to right them. And in turn, he'd been taken for a ride. Not just him, but poor Dawes, too.

It made him furious.

Furious enough to act.

A brief thought raced through his mind. He worried Daniel would sense it too. But his brother seemed too caught up on his speech to read Jonathan's thoughts.

It was the hopeful semblance of a plan, all depending on whatever reserves of energy he could muster. He tried moving his right arm. Doing so was a challenge—his limbs felt asleep. He started with the shoulder, rolling it until it sprung alive with a shock of pins and needles. It hurt, but hell, it was something. He worked down his arm, tensing at the elbow. Moving his fingers felt impossible but still he strained, burning his reserves down to near nothing.

And as his consciousness flickered in and out, he made a fist.

Daniel stopped. His speech paused, and he watched his brother suspiciously. Jonathan closed his eyes, pretending to lose consciousness. He heard Daniel release a smug grunt and continued pacing about the shack.

Carefully as possible, Jonathan reached to his pant pocket.

A frantic determination overtook him once he grasped the handle of his straight razor.

Daniel froze again. A cold amalgam of humor and uncertainty overtook his voice.

"What are you thinking, Jon?"

Jonathan acted fast, pulling the razor free and extracting the blade. Daniel responded faster, sensing Jonathan's moves and bear-hugging him before he could bring the blade up.

"*You little pest,*" he hissed.

Jonathan struggled in Daniel's grip. His brother's hold was crushing, threatening to break his grasp on the blade. He squirmed to no success.

Daniel's voice dripped with hate. "Did you really think you could get one up on me? That I wouldn't notice your intent? Not only are you weak, Jon. You're a damn fool."

He still fought, even as his energy waned, his lights dimming further. Daniel's hold remained tight, but as Jonathan flailed, he found room. Gripping the knife, he pushed his arm away from his own thigh and closer to Daniel's. A swell of hope sprung in his chest as a sliver of uncertainty radiated from his brother. He stretched himself to his limit, reaching Daniel's leg with the blade.

He angled the straight razor's sharp edge and sliced through Daniel's nylons, cutting into flesh.

A brief worry crossed his mind. Could Daniel feel pain in his current form? A clenched hiss emanating from between his brother's teeth answered his question. Instinctively, Daniel released his hold and clamped his palm over the slash.

Jonathan took advantage of the moment.

He raised the blade and ran its edge across Daniel's throat.

Daniel let loose a shocked bellow. The slice had been lucky, opening stitches uniting Bingus' head to Antonio's body. Jonathan felt his brother's knees buckle, threatening to topple. The gash in his throat yawned like a mouth, emitting a viscous black ooze. Daniel's focus shifted from his brother to his new wounds. One hand clasped his torn thigh, the other his opened throat. He stumbled forward, his gait clumsy and pained.

As Daniel's resolve faltered, a surge of strength returned to Jonathan. His ankles wobbled against the floor as he tried to stand, slashing at Daniel's hand with the blade. His brother yelled, releasing his neck, swinging a bloodied fist at his brother's head. The panicked, sloppy blow grazed off Jonathan's temple with minimal effect. Jonathan grabbed onto a loose loop of fishing wire hanging from Daniel's throat and pulled, further opening the wound. The black sepsis blasted free, accompanied by the stench of rotting meat.

Daniel yelled, then charged, ramming Jonathan into the wall of the shack. The worn boards fragmented, shooting bolts of pain up Jonathan's spine. His blade hand darted upward, splitting Daniel's cheek, freeing more rot. He tugged harder at the fishing wire, unraveling the makeshift stitches.

"*You're ruining everything!*" Daniel hissed.

"Fuck you, *brother*," Jonathan responded, returning the razor to Daniel's throat.

Daniel charged Jonathan into a second wall, then another. Clouds of rotted sawdust filled the air, stinging Jonathan's eyes. He remained on the offensive, tearing wire, slashing skin. Daniel's balance teetered as the wire further unwound, yet he still treated his brother like a battering ram. He blindly slammed Jonathan against the shack door, which splintered at the hinges and gave away. The brothers careened through the threshold and into the rainy night.

With one foot into the muck Daniel slipped, falling forward. Jonathan landed back-first into the cold mud. His sibling sprawled atop him, knocking the breath from his lungs. Daniel wasted no time fighting for dominance, wrapping hands around Jonathan's neck and squeezing.

"Go to hell, Jon," he wheezed. The rot oozing from his neck splashed Jonathan in the face, inciting a riot in his gut.

Jonathan's face burnt with a fading panic. Daniel's grip had grown weak while his strength had returned tenfold. He grabbed Daniel's wrists and broke their hold, then rolled to the left. The two wheel-barrowed through muck until Jonathan pinned his brother to the ground.

"See you there, *brother*," he said, bringing the straight razor to the remaining wire and cutting.

The fight left Antonio's former body once Jonathan separated the head. Jonathan stood, weakness retreating like a great sigh. He squinted at the corpse from the corner of his eye. It twitched spasmodically in the mud, like a child in the throes of a minor seizure. Jonathan spat on it and turned away.

The head attached to him hissed silently, gnashing its jaws in some pathetic attempt to bite.

"You fool," Daniel's voice echoed inside Jonathan's head. *"You utter fool. Do you really think this stopped anything? Dawes must be in the cemetery by now, dooming this town for eternity. There's no way can you stop him in time."* Daniel emitted a wet, throaty chuckle. *"You're bound to fail, Jon."*

Jonathan ignored his brother's taunting. He had to reach Dawes. He knew chances were slim, but he had to try, damn it.

He positioned himself so he faced the road sideways. He stared at the path ahead of him with the corner of his eye and started sidestepping his way toward town, Daniel jeering the entire way.

D awes relit the candle and started the incantation from the top. His nose, eyes, and throat burnt from the fragrant smoke billowing off the wormwood. The coat draped above him had soaked through, laying waste to his flimsy cover. Blood pulsed from the bite marks on his finger stumps. Crimson splotches rendered sections of words on his spell sheet near-illegible. But by his seventh attempt, he had a firm grasp on the ruined passages. His voice quivered from the cold and the pain as he worked through the last sections.

"Encanda, tsumanac, ressurectum d'amore," he read, "tsunafra consequa, d'onofrio venupta, veulovria consac…"

Tears streamed from his eyes, blurring his vision. He pictured Marcie and a less lonely life. He soldiered through the misery.

"Conentia nervosa, vibranca delirius. Vorivica ultum, corvonka atonis…"

He stopped as the ground rumbled beneath him. It was the type of tremor one could sleep through peacefully, stopping as soon as it started. An odd sound followed—a feminine voice, moaning in either lust or pain. Dawes' heart raced, his pulse throbbing in his skull.

Shaking in anticipation, he began the incantation's last passage.

JONATHAN WISHED HE HAD HIS WALKING CANES. EVEN WITH his newfound adrenaline, he struggled to stay upright. Daniel's taunting didn't help matters.

"Jonathan Crabb, the world's most knock-kneed hero!" He cackled. *"Could save the day in time, if just maybe he could walk in a straight line!"*

"Shut up, you," Jonathan said, grabbing Daniel by Bingus' hair. Using the razor, he began carving the stitches binding them together. He sliced into his horn and snarled in pain. A slurry of blood sprayed down his face. His legs wobbled, threatening to give.

He stumbled onward.

Voices echoed somewhere down the road—cheers and screams. Lanterns glowed in his peripherals, their distance anybody's guess. Jonathan stumbled closer, hacking away at the head attached to him.

If I get him off, I might make it, he thought.

"Fat fucking chance," Daniel countered.

Jonathan stopped his trek and focused on slashing at the wire, yelling every time he sloughed away his own skin. He tugged on the attached head, his heart racing faster with every centimeter the fishing line gave. The sounds of the cheering crowd faded under the dull thud of his temples. He fell to his knees and sawed away at the conjoining spot with a strength he'd never known prior.

He screamed in triumph when he tore the head free.

"Rot in hell, you bastard!" he yelled, and threw Daniel/Bingus' head into the mud. He wiped blood from his eyes and climbed to his feet.

Ahead, the entire populace of Spudsville froze in shock. Silence consumed the congregation, save for the incensed snort of a fighting hog. Jonathan stared back, a cold sweat dampening his brow.

"Well…" he said, stumbling over words. "I suppose this doesn't look too good."

Otis stepped out from a corroded awning covering a makeshift bar. He walked over to the head, grabbed it by the hair, and stared at it. His glare turned to Jonathan, who shifted uncomfortably.

"He—he's alive," Jonathan said, his voice desperate. "He's evil! What he's started—what he's set in motion… we have to get to the graveyard, before it's too late! Please…you have to—"

"Murderer," Otis growled, eyes lit with rage. An incensed thrall rose from the crowd.

"We've got a killer in our ranks!" yelled Merrick, who stepped over scraps of General Grace's child soldiers and took position next to Otis. "A regular goddamn freak, from the looks of it."

General Grace stood next to Merrick; two rivals united by disdain. Her two remaining fighters crouched on all fours beside her wooden legs, their skin split by cuts and abrasions. They growled at Jonathan, bearing jagged teeth.

"Damn criminal!" Grace yelled. She wiped the blood of her fallen troops from her brow. "What lowlife kills a mime?"

A dreadful anxiety weighed down Jonathan's gut. The

whole crowd lurched away from the fighting ring and surrounded him from all sides.

"You have to believe me…" he tried as hands grabbed him, forcing his arms behind his back. Any hope left in him withered.

From the center of the crowd waddled Eunice, who stopped a foot away from Jonathan and stared him down.

"Well," she said, running a finger through the blood caking his face. "Doesn't seem we need a trial, do we?"

A violent outcry ripped from the crowd as Otis held Daniel/Bingus' head high.

"In that case, I say we take the killer to the tracks. Give him a proper Spudsville goodbye."

Erupting in agreement, the mob lifted Jonathan above their heads. They carried him screaming down Main Street, away from the graveyard, toward the train tracks.

Daniel chuckled icily somewhere inside Jonathan's brain.

THE MOANS INCREASED WHEN DAWES REACHED THE FINAL words of the incantation. A bright heat radiated from the ground beneath him, turning his makeshift shelter into a sauna. The quakes continued like the violent thud of a clogged artery. He winced through the blinding smoke and recited the spell's conclusion.

"Dona Consecto, Venta resurrectus mi amore, Marcie Klein!"

The earth settled and the moaning stopped. The candle and the wormwood simultaneously extinguished as the ground beneath him cooled. Even the rain falling around him ceased. Dawes removed the soaked coat from atop him and stared out at a world suddenly cast into peace. The silence around him was broken only by the succession of his rattled breaths.

He waited for something, *anything,* to happen.

Then all at once, hell ascended onto earth.

The woman's voice returned, not as a moan but a brutal attack on Dawes' eardrums. He yelped as the skillet heat of the ground beneath him blistered his knees. Dawes bolted from the ground, frantically back-stepping from Marcie's grave. A seismic blast of city-leveling proportions hit the earth, sending him sprawling. The back of his head thumped against moist earth. Heat scorched his neck. He shrieked, staggering to his feet.

The ground surrounding Marcie's grave exploded, toppling him once more.

❦

THE INCREASING TREMORS THREATENED TO LEVEL JONATHAN onto the tracks. A few of the townsfolk murmured in concern before redirecting their attention back to him. They growled in spite, glaring at him with accusing eyes.

To his left stood Eunice, Sal, and Merrick, and between them, their fighting pig. To his right, General Grace towered above her two remaining soldiers. The remaining township split into two separate groups behind them all. The message was clear; leaving the tracks meant being gored by either hog or child. Being pulverized by a loco-motive was a mercy in comparison.

Folks had drawn straws to determine who'd do the sentencing, for legalities sake. Otis won. He stood closest to the tracks, his normally unaffected nature replaced by disappointment and disgust.

"We let you inta our community, all those years ago," he said, his voice wet with spite. "Gave ya a job. Shelter. Little did we know, we were housin' a monster." He stopped, snorted, and spit a lunger onto the tracks by Jonathan's feet. "Jonathan Crabb, for the crime of de-headin' a mime, we sentence you ta *death by train!*"

The township burst into vigilant cheering. Jonathan's heart sank. Somewhere in the far distance, someone—something—let loose a hellish scream. Jonathan scanned the crowd to see if anyone else noticed, but they were too lost in their rage.

SOMETHING BURST FROM MARCIE'S GRAVE, RISING INTO THE dull sky above him. It settled twenty feet above the ground, floating in menacing glory. Dawes froze, mortified. It was a beast even the darkest parts of his mind couldn't conjure. Its wings were fine skeletal models, the span rivaling a jumbo jet. Scraps of expired flesh hung off the jagged bones like tattered remains of an old sail. The thing's massive, furry body reminded Dawes of a moth's midsection. Claws sprouted from the ends of long skeletal legs extending from its lower half. Six long, scaly stalks sprouted from its torso, writhing about like snakes. Attached to each stalk was a head, the features of each identical. Long blonde hair flowed off their scalps. Dawes stared at the familiar faces and screamed louder than he ever had before.

Marcie's face.

Six of them.

The beauty he remembered was trumped by the malice in her eyes. The Marcie heads opened their gnashing jaws and screamed with raw intensity. Blue flames burst from their mouths, reaching the muck surrounding Dawes. The heat singed the hairs on his head. The beast's long tail extended, slashing at the ground before him with a sharp, scythe-shaped tip, flinging earth high into the air.

Dawes' paralysis broke as instinct kicked in, screaming *get away get away get the fuck away.* He jumped to his feet, spun around, and ran as fast as he could. The Marcie heads screamed behind him. Something grabbed him, and before he knew it, the thing lifted him in its claws. It carried him ten, fifteen, twenty feet into the air, then tossed him like a ragdoll. Dawes soared like a small, coasting vessel, watching the gravestones transition into ragged copses of trees.

And like a small vessel he descended, hitting the ground hard. His vision went red and static. A bone in his chest snapped—ribs, collarbone, *something.* He barrel-rolled through the mud, each rotation sending another shock of pain throughout his being. He came to a stop and emitted something between a groan and a sob.

Above him, the thing circled. Dawes watched it, antici-pating its descent, ready for it to tear him apart. Instead, the thing waited. The Marcie faces sneered at him. The look in their eyes challenged him to stand. They were playing with him; having fun with their prey before going in for the kill.

Dawes debated laying there, letting the cold do him in, or waiting until the beast decided to finish him off.

He realized he didn't have the patience to wait. Winc-ing, he stood and resumed his retreat.

JONATHAN HEARD ANOTHER SHRIEK IN THE DISTANCE. MORE tremors jolted the ground beneath them. He thought about Dawes and felt deep worry.

Some townies shared troubled glances at the continual quakes and distant screams. A different sound erupted behind him, commandeering most of their attentions, bringing vocal cheers:

The squeal of a train.

DAWES RAN FASTER THAN EVER BEFORE, DESPITE HIS BODY crying out in protest. Everything hurt. But every side-eyed glance at the thing approaching behind him was incentive to keep going.

The thing remained a leisurely distance behind him. Occasionally it swooped in close, blasting his surroundings with flames before backing away, its heads cackling in amusement.

Or it would grab him once more and toss, sending him careening. With every throw he felt less human and more like a sack of broken glass. He wished the thing would just end him, for crying out loud.

He made it to downtown Spudsville, hoping the crowd was still assembled. Maybe they could help—strength in numbers or something. Maybe the sight of the devilish Marcie hell-beast was exactly what the township needed to expel their collective funk, band together, and *do something*.

But downtown was empty again, save for the slaughtered remains of General Grace's soldiers.

Fuck.

The sound of a massive explosion behind Dawes

caught him further off guard. He spun around and was met with the feeling of hope sinking abysmally lower.

The Marcie-beast coasted down the empty street; its massive wingspan extended. Jagged bones sheered through the abandoned storefronts. Buildings collapsed behind the thing, raining the street with brick and mortar debris.

If Spudsville was already on its deathbed, then the Marcie-beast was the grim reaper.

The beast bulleted toward Dawes, who dove down as it neared. In the moment before collision it jetted into the sky, engulfing Dawes in clouds of emulsified brick and detritus. He coughed and sputtered, gagging on the refuse. He fumbled back onto his feet and continued onward, blinded by the inorganic dust polluting the air. Somewhere above or behind him, the Marcie-beast continued its awful screeching.

And somewhere ahead of him, Dawes heard another sound.

Voices, in the distance. In the direction of the train tracks.

Was that…cheering?

Stumbling through the pollution, Dawes picked up his pace. He had to find help. Had to find the crowds.

Onward he pushed, out of the demolished downtown streets and toward the train tracks.

JUDGING BY ITS SOUND, THE TRAIN WAS CLOSING DISTANCE. Deep in the night, behind the dead bushes, Jonathan could see the dim glow of an approaching headlight. His blood froze to slush. *This is the end,* he thought.

"See you soon," Daniel taunted, his lingering voice but a whisper in Jonathan's head.

"You saying your prayers, freak?" asked Merrick. "Time's winding down. Maybe a few Hail Mary's will get you a spot in the good place."

"Unlikely," General Grace said.

Jonathan shuddered, falling to his knees. *I'm sorry, Lord, if you exist.* He wiped tears from his face. *I'm sorry, Dawes, for getting you involved in this shit. Daniel, if I'd appreciated you then, we wouldn't be here in the first place.*

Oh god. I'm so, so sorry.

The train grew nearer. Jonathan shut his eyes and awaited its arrival, hoping he wouldn't feel much pain.

To his left, someone familiar screamed. He opened his eyes and looked. The Spudsvillians surrounding him followed suit.

A lanky figure burst through the copse of dead trees, mud slathering his slim frame like a second skin. Gone was the wispy hair providing sparse foliage to his scalp. He kept his left hand—what was left of it—curled at his side. Each step he took was an awkward wobble threatening collapse.

"Dawes!" Jonathan shouted.

Dawes made it to the crowd before face-planting into the mud. The onlookers watched him with the vague curiosity of finding unusual roadkill. Otis approached him, nudging Dawes' still body with his boot.

"What in heavens happened ta ya?"

Dawes leaned up, resting on his forearms, fighting for breath. He stumbled through a panicked explanation, gibberish save for certain words. The graveyard. A beast. Wings and fire. Downtown.

Marcie.

"Marcie?" Otis said. "Who the hell's Marcie?"

"You…you know…" Dawes panted. "…*My* Marcie."

From behind the trees came a screech, then a loud boom. The entire township jumped and screamed. Something burst from the copse, something *giant*, reducing the dead trees into a shower of splinters. Onlookers shrank, covering themselves from the chunks of wood raining onto them.

The beast rocketed into the sky and descended, stopping fifteen feet above the ground. The simple sight of it made Jonathan's mind break. Of all the twisted things he'd seen recently, this—this *creature*—was by far the worst.

Dawes climbed to his feet and scampered closer to the tracks.

"M-Marcie!" he yelled, pointing with a shaky hand. "For the love of fuck, Marcie!"

Panicked, the majority of the township hurried to the side of the track opposite the beast. Only a select few remained—Merrick and Eunice, with Boss Hog at their side. General Grace joined them, her soldiers in tow. Otis remained, stunned, his own faith—or lack thereof—tested.

"What the fuck d'ya want?" Merrick yelled. Unease betrayed his usual bullheadedness. Unresponsive, the thing glared at the congregation with its twelve eyes. Merrick continued.

"You come in peace? You come in war? Say something, you fuckin' freak!"

"Don't piss it off!" Someone yelled. Merrick ignored the request.

Jonathan left the track once certain the attention had shifted from him. Dawes approached, falling to his knees. Jonathan grabbed his friend, helping him up.

"My god, Dawes, I'm so sorry," he whispered in his ear. Dawes sputtered and huffed, fighting to respond.

"We *need* to leave."

At the frontline, Merrick found his usual boisterous courage. "You gonna do anything, you giant floating pussy? Or are you just gonna watch us like some voyeur?"

The thing descended a foot closer to the earth, yet still didn't act.

Merrick sneered. "Figures. All bark and no bite. Probably couldn't stand a fight against Grace's sissy battalion."

General Grace scowled. "Hey," she said with offense.

"No way you could handle a round with Boss Hog here," Merrick said. Eunice nodded, slapping the swine on its ass. Boss Hog took attack position, kicking mud with its hooves, bearing fangs and releasing a battle-hardened squeal. "No sir, this hog's shat out things scarier than you, you cryptid fuck—"

The Marcie-heads opened their mouths and screamed, launching bursts of fiery breath in Boss Hog's direction. The pig squealed, thrashing as the flames torched its skin. The scent of barbecue saturated the air. Merrick screamed.

"Not the fucking pig!"

The rain extinguished the flames, but the damage was done. Boss Hog writhed in the mud, the sound leaving its snout worse than anything Jonathan had ever heard. Merrick charged toward his prized hog, yelling a storm.

The Marcie-beast whipped its long tail forward. The scythe end caught Merrick under the groin and sliced upward with ease, exiting the top of his head. Merrick froze in place, sputtering, his eyes overtaken with absolute disbelief.

The township began screaming as his body bifurcated into jagged, uneven halves, each part collapsing lifelessly opposite each other. A mess of entrails spilled out of his split cavity, steaming in the cold.

The Spudsvillians broke into a frenzied anarchy, running each other down while trying to escape. Jonathan watched them all, wide-eyed, paralyzed in his own terror.

General Grace stumbled backward in shock. She stepped wrong, and her left leg splintered beneath her. She fell gracelessly into the mud with a grunt.

"Get it!" She yelled at her two remaining soldiers.

The androgynous troops charged the Marcie Beast, grasping onto the tail dangling above the ground. Avoiding its scythe-end, they scaled it with ease. They attacked with their jagged teeth and claws, drawing streams of black blood from the beast's flesh. Unfazed by their assault, the Marcie-beast swung its tail upward, toward the faces growing from its midsection. The sprouted necks of the Marcie-heads accreted from its torso, and the children were greeted by gnashing, serrated teeth. Three heads took to each child, tearing, ripping and feasting. Blood, scraps of flesh, and bone rained down on General Grace, who screamed in abject terror. She awkwardly scooted through the sludge, trying to escape fate. The Marcie-beast descended, grabbing the general's head with razor-sharp claws. It pulled, and General Grace's head popped off in its grasp. Gore sluiced from her neck as her body sank into the mud, twitching in the throes of death.

The heads finished crunching on the marrow of General Grace's soldiers and faced the panicked Spudsvillians. With a furious shriek, it started on the rest of them.

DAWES SCREAMED WHEN BOLTS OF FIRE SUBMERGED BOTH Eunice and Otis, cooking them alive. As the thing swooped down he crouched, expecting it to sweep him up and finish him. Instead it glided to the other side of the tracks, into the bellowing township.

A train squealed in the distance, stealing his attention.

An idea jogged through his mind. Everything became circular. How he arrived, how he'll leave. He turned to Jonathan, who still looked petrified.

"You ever jump a train before?"

Pale-faced, Jonathan shook his head.

"Well, there's a first time for everything." Still on his knees, Dawes turned his back to Jonathan. "Climb on. We're getting out of here."

Jonathan hesitated, staring at Dawes like he was crazy. The sound of the screams on the other side of the track put a fire under his rear, and he wrapped his arms around Dawes' shoulders.

Dawes stood, wincing. Everything still hurt. His legs threatened to buckle under Jonathan's weight. Yet he managed, his slow walk increasing into a run. Behind him, the train approached.

He chanced a glance to the other side of the tracks, to the unfolding bloodbath. The Marcie-beast moved with ease, tearing the township of Spudsville to shreds then charring those remnants with its fire breath. The terrified screams decreased with the dwindling population.

Once Spudsville was gone, who would the Marcie-beast turn its rage toward?

He focused his attention to the oncoming train. The locomotive sped by. He wondered what the conductor thought of the unfolding massacre. Were such occurrences common to someone touring this mess of a world? From the bottom of his heart, he hoped not.

Despite his body pleading him to give up, Dawes kept his pace. Rusty boxcars passed; their doors shut tight. A deep worry sank in his stomach—could he do this? *Could he?*

Hope blossomed at the sight of an empty car, the lip of its open door shoulder-height to Dawes. A metal winch stuck up from the floor, begging him to grab on. He had never hopped a speeding train. Heard even the thought of doing so was simply preposterous. But given their situation, the preposterous was their only hope.

With a defiant yell he jumped toward the boxcar, grabbing the winch with his one good hand. Behind him, Jonathan screamed, clutching onto Dawes' neck for dear life.

Immediately, Dawes regretted his decision.

The speed of the train wrecked his balance, throwing his legs out from under him. They swung dangerously close to the train's spinning wheels. This was no good—no good at all. His whole pathetic life flashed before his eyes while he simultaneously envisioned himself and Jonathan being reduced to a paste on the train tracks. Just like Marcie, and the many before her. His grip slipped on the winch. Death came calling.

Jonathan screamed louder than hell itself before going quiet.

"Forgive me, Jon," Dawes said as his hold started to release.

Two grubby hands reached out from the boxcar and grabbed his arm before he slipped under the wheels.

"Hold on!" Someone yelled from inside the car. With

two beefy arms, the stranger yanked Dawes halfway inside. Dawes reinstated his hold on the winch, took a deep breath, and with the stranger's help, crawled inside the boxcar.

"Whoa, Nelly!" the stranger yelled, falling backward as he finished pulling Dawes inside. "That was a close one!"

Dawes rolled onto his back, his pulse jackhammering his brain. It felt as if a heart attack could take him any moment. He looked outside the boxcar's open door and watched the world speed by in a blur. He let out a relieved laugh as his heartbeat steadied.

"We made it, Jon," he said. "We actually fucking made it." He laughed harder.

Jonathan said nothing. Dawes turned to an empty space behind him.

"Your little friend wasn't so lucky," said a somber voice.

The man who pulled him in sat upright, elbows planted on his knees. Grime crusted his massive beard and the patches of worn skin surrounding it. He wiped his hands on the ragged clothes draping his frame and removed his dusty hat. A look of remorse stained his cloudy eyes.

"Little fella fell off your back. From what it sounded like, went straight under the wheels. You're lucky you didn't join him."

Dawes, shot up and leaned his head outside of the moving boxcar, hoping he could see Jonathan chasing after the speeding train, far behind but whole and well. All he saw was the dark night behind him. The sound of the train passing through the night was deafening, yet in the distance he still heard the Marcie-beast's shrieks.

Dawes fell onto his ass, shocked. A dull ache began gnawing at his stomach.

Dear god. Jon.

The man behind him spoke, his voice an incoherent muffle. Dawes turned toward him, mouth agape. The vagrant repeated himself with a look of concern.

"I said, what happened to you? You look like you've been through hell."

Dawes tried to respond, but his words came out a sob.

EPILOGUE

Later

Another day finished.

Dawes flopped onto the single mattress with a heavy groan, his whole weight sinking against the springs. His limbs ached—hell, they always ached, but a day of labor in the fields made everything worse. While better than standing, even the simple act of laying hurt.

He stared at the cracked ceiling above him, focusing on the phallic water stain bleeding through the fissure. A stream of sweat leaked down his forehead, and he wished for a fan to make his shack more habitable. His current abode made Jonathan's look like a palace—this place barely held a mattress, icebox, footlocker and hotplate, much less the world's loneliest sad sack.

A fly buzzed, landing on the space between Dawes' eyes. He swatted at it, stopping before making a terrible mistake—it had been ages since the infection had taken the rest of his left hand, yet he still hadn't grown used to the hook. This negligence left scars across his worn face, costing him a substantial chunk of his nose. If he'd looked ugly before, he was downright monstrous now.

The hardships of yesterday seemed like a blessing in hindsight.

A year had passed since he'd jumped that train, and while the subsequent passing days felt like epochs, the ache of losing Jon remained fresh. Not a moment passed where he didn't feel the pain, no matter the distance between himself and Spudsville.

For the first month he stuck with Trevor, the derelict on the train. Most of the time Dawes stayed in a saddened haze, dulling the agony with homemade, high-proof corn mash. He couldn't remember much more than the passing of the outside world from the door of an open boxcar, the sound of his own sobs, and Trevor's clear discomfort over the situation. The bender ended with waking under the shelter of dead brush, Trevor nowhere in sight. Once again, Dawes was left to his devices.

He continued further South, mostly on foot. Found odd work in time-lost towns with names he never bothered learning. Every time he felt like he could settle down, something would call him to hit the road again. Normally it involved word of a flying beast making a steady trek from the north, tearing through Podunk towns in search of *something*. For most of the varied townships, the Marcie-beast sounded like some ham-fisted myth. Dawes never stuck around long enough for them to learn of its horrible reality.

He anchored himself in a dilapidated little hole called Scrub Brush, where he'd never planned to stay for longer than a few weeks. Funny how life works. When looking for work he found a job at an okra farm run by another familiar face from his past—Lobster Hands, who'd found moderate success as a farmer in the years after the sideshow folded. Lobster Hands paid Dawes decently, providing free boarding as well. It was by no means glamorous—the work was hard, and Lobster Hands was unafraid to pinch when he felt his workers were slacking. But Dawes grew comfortable as time passed without word of Marcie-beast, and compared to feeding Eunice's and Sal's hogs, the hard work still felt like a vacation.

The fly left his face and lingered above him, frenzied, waiting for the opportunity to dive-bomb him. Dawes sighed and slapped it away with his right hand. The pest was unrelenting. *For the best*, Dawes supposed. He couldn't get too comfortable—he still had too much to do. Ignoring his bodies groan, he stood from the mattress and walked to his footlocker. Bent down and spun the combo lock, unlatching it with a three-number code. He opened its small olive-colored door and removed the objects:

Wormwood.

Candles.

The straight razor.

The book.

He'd found it at the end of an exhausting day spent digging through dirt with a dull trowel, coming up short on his daily okra quota. He'd been fighting to keep his eyes open, daydreaming about collapsing on his mattress and never waking up, when the trowel's tip hit something hard. He'd half-anticipated another coffin lid—lord knows he'd dug up his fair share already—but on further inspection he found something shockingly familiar. He knew there was no way stumbling upon it could be coincidence.

The very particular straight razor beneath the book was too telling.

He knew better than to take it—the troubles caused by the grimoire were still fresh in his mind. Yet still he found himself placing it in his footlocker that same night. And as the days passed, he found himself removing it after his shift's ends and studying its passages, his fear of its foreboding power being replaced with curiosity. Excitement, too, of knowing what it could fix.

It could end the guilt he couldn't shake.

Dawes placed the candles in the appropriate position on the floor—East, South, North, West. He dug a lighter from his pocket and lit their wicks, along with the wormwood. Smoke exhumed the small shack. Dawes lay Jonathan's straight razor in the middle of the lit candles, opened the grimoire to the right passage, and began the passage as he'd translated in Scrub Brush's old town library.

"Colprizana, offina alta nuestra, fuara menut. Ego autem mortuus sum: In quo quaeris Jonathan Crabb, et motrui sunt quaerite me."

Something creaked inside the small shack; something like a foot on an old floorboard, or a sad moan. Jonathan shook, continuing with the spell.

"Jonathan Crabb spiritus Pomponius ducta defunctus est et nunc Veritam accedre ad hanc portam, et exaudi precam meam. Berald, beroald, Balbin, Gab, Gabor, Agaba! Surge, et ego invocabo te, et arguer!"

He then brought his hook to his right palm, and as per the spell's instructions, opened the skin. He held his hand out over Jonathan's straight razor and let the blood spill onto it. He extinguished the lit candles. Blew out the wormwood. Lowered his head, and began to meditate.

Come back to me, Jon, he thought.
Come back, and we'll never be alone again.

The End

ACKNOWLEDGMENTS

A million wet kisses go to Sam Richard, without whom this book would not be possible. Thank you for always giving me a chance, seeing something in my writing worth pursuing. And for being such a good friend. Special thanks to Neal Auch, Don Noble and S.C. Burke for collectively making this book *look* stunning. And a big tip of the fedora to Garrett Cook, whose writing workshops helped facilitate the start of this weird little novella.

The best part about writing isn't the books, but the amazing people you meet. Thank you to the following folks for the friendship, guidance and support: Sam, Brendan, Charles and Mark, Katy Michelle Quinn, Danger Slater, Michael Kazepis, Tiffany Scandal, Constance Anne Fitzgerald, Emma Johnson, Max Booth III, Mona Swan LeSueur, and countless others. Special thanks to Brian Lewis and Kyle Kulseth for always providing honest feedback on my terrible first drafts.

A big thank you to Kass, for everything. You have my heart.

And thank you for reading this.

- Jo

ABOUT THE AUTHOR

Jo Quenell lives in Washington State and writes sometimes. The Mud Ballad is her first novella.

ALSO BY WEIRDPUNK BOOKS

Sabbath of the Fox-Devils by Sam Richard

After learning about the existence of a powerful grimoire through a cartoon, 12-year-old Joe is determined to find it and change his lot in life. But in doing so, he'll also uncover a local priest's dark secret and how it may be connected to Joe's brother abruptly leaving town five years ago.

Part homage to the small-creature horror films of the 80s (*Ghoulies, Gremlins, The Gate*) and part Splatterpunk take on a Goosebumps book, *Sabbath of the Fox-Devils* is a weird, diabolical coming-of-age horror story of self-liberation in an oppressive religious environment set during the Satanic Panic.

Prepare your soul to revel in the darkness.

"Light the black candles and invert the cross as Sam Richard conjures a coming-of-age story of Satanic panic, creature carnage, and blasphemous terror!"

— RYAN HARDING (*GENITAL GRINDER*)

The New Flesh: A Literary Tribute to David Cronenberg - Edited by Sam Richard and Brendan Vidito

Videodrome. Scanners. The Brood. Crash. The Fly. The films of David Cronenberg have haunted and inspired generations. His name has become synonymous with the body horror subgenere and the term "Cronenbergian" has been used to describe the stark, grotesque, and elusive quality of his work. These eighteen stories bring his themes and ideas into the present, throbbing with unnatural life.

A Splatterpunk Awards nominee for Best Anthology, The New Flesh features stories by Brain Evenson, Gwendolyn Kiste, Cody Goodfellow, Katy Michelle Quinn, Ryan Harding, and more. Plus an introduction by the legendary Kathe Koja!

Zombie Punks Fuck Off - Edited by Sam Richard

(Co-published with CLASH Books)

We've been hearing forever that punk is dead. And zombie stories are even deader. *Zombie Punks Fuck Off* is here to show that is bullshit. This anthology is loaded with 14 stories of gnawing teeth, shredded entrails, rotting masses, punk as fuck fury, post-punk weirdness, and beautiful decay.

Featuring stories by Danger Slater, Emma Alice Johnson, David W. Barbee, Carmilla Voiez, Asher Ellis, and more.

"This is my dream book. I can't believe it exists!"

— JEFF BURK, AUTHOR OF
SHATNERQUAKE AND *THE VERY
INEFFECTIVE HAUNTED HOUSE*

Hybrid Moments: A Literary Tribute to the Misfits - Edited by Sam Richard and Emma Alice Johnson

You know the songs. They're etched into every punk's brain. Not just because they're catchy, but because there's something else there. Glenn Danzig's lyrics evoke intense imagery. Beautiful, dark, monster imagery. There's poetry between the whoa-oh-ohs. There are stories in those songs. They just need to be told.

And now, some of underground fiction's most talented fiends have. Featuring stories by: David Agranoff, José Cruz, Darci Schummer, Nicholaus Patnaude, and more.

Hybrid Moments: A Literary Tribute to the Misfits will force you to see this timeless horror punk in a completely different light.